# DEATH ON
# THE CAMPUS

# DEATH ON THE CAMPUS

## ADDISON SIMMONS

**COACHWHIP PUBLICATIONS**
Greenville, Ohio

*Death on the Campus*, by Addison Simmons
© 2018 Coachwhip Publications

Addison Simmons (1902-1972)
Published 1935.
No claims made on public domain material.
Introduction © Curtis Evans
Cover: Yankton College Conservatory, SD (LoC)

CoachwhipBooks.com

ISBN 1-61646-455-0
ISBN-13 978-1-61646-455-4

# INTRODUCTION

ORIGINAL DUSTJACKET FOR
*DEATH ON THE CAMPUS*

# ANOTHER PLAYER IN THE MYSTERY BAND:
## The Crime Fiction of Addison Simmons
## CURTIS EVANS

The contribution of Addison Simmons (1902-1972) to detective fiction is scanty, consisting, evidently, of but two mystery titles, which were separated by more than a decade: *Death on the Campus* (1935) and *Dead Weight* (1946). Yet beyond his being the author of a pair of detective novels, "Ad," as Simmons was known to his friends, was a prolific professional writer of both short stories and radio plays and a talented musician who as a student at Harvard served as the second director of the University Band. Like his vastly more famous contemporary John Dickson Carr (1906-1977) and such other recently reprinted mystery writers of merit as Todd Downing (1902-1974), Clifford Orr (1899-1951), Evelyn Page (1902-1977) and Dorothy Blair (1903-1976), Ad Simmons is representative of a group of bright, young American college men and women from the Jazz Age for whom a fondness for detective fiction in its bountiful Golden Era (the period, roughly, between the two world wars) served as an entrée—often short-lived, to be sure—into novel writing. Only recently, with the revival of interest in vintage mystery, have we really begun to appreciate the extent of the entertaining legacy left us by these young detective fiction enthusiasts of eighty or ninety years ago, many of whom played but briefly in the mystery band and only now are being rediscovered.

Ad Simmons was born Adolph Sylvan Simmons (Ad seems to have changed his name to Addison while a student at Harvard) in Boston on April 9, 1902, to Jacob and Dora Kramer Simmons,

Russian Jews from partitioned Poland who migrated to the United States in the 1890s. The proprietor of a barbershop, Jacob quickly prospered in the United States. By 1910 he and Dora, a milliner, had moved with their four children—Adolph and two additional sons, Arthur Max and Eliot Daniel, as well as a daughter, Rosalie—into one floor of a recently completed triple-decker apartment house at 128 King Street in Dorchester. (Between 1870 and 1920 over 15,000 thousand triple-decker apartment houses were erected in Boston, particularly in such "streetcar suburbs" as Dorchester, Roxbury, Mattapan, and Jamaica Plain, where as an alternative to tenement and row housing they proved quite popular with the city's emerging middle class.) Jacob passed away at the age of 50 in 1921, but in the 'Twenties Ad attended Harvard University and Harvard Law School and his elder brother, Arthur, Tufts University and Tufts University School of Medicine. While Arthur became a physician, however, Ad, blessed—or cursed as some would see it—with artistic temperament, followed a different and more precarious career path, as did his younger brother, Eliot, who played in an orchestra, and his sister, Rosalie, who graced the stage as a dancer.

Ad quickly evinced wayward artistic tendencies at Harvard, seemingly spending most of his time there immersed in music. Not only did he serve as the college's band director, he wrote his own compositions, such as "Harvard's Own March," and formed his own jazz orchestra, which he dubbed "Addison Simmons' Collegians." The Harvard Band and the Collegians accepted engagements at events around New England, including, for example, the Collegians in 1926 at the Radcliffe Catholic Club's annual dance and the Band in 1923 at the annual Worcester, Massachusetts, concert and dance held at the Hotel Bancroft under the auspices of the Worcester Harvard Club. At the latter affair the band's program included John Philip Sousa's *El Capitan*, Camille Saint-Saens' *The Swan*, Edvard Grieg's Triumphal March from *Sigurd Jorsalfar*, and the Finale of Pyotr Ilyich Tchaikovsky's Symphony No. 4.[1]

In his press publicity as an author in the 1930s, Ad later stated that he had "'fathered' the University Band, in its formative period after the War," which seems a fair enough claim. An advocate of formation marching, which enjoyed a surge of popularity with college and high school bands after the First World War, Ad in a letter to the *Harvard Crimson* defended what he termed "the practice of performing maneuvers" against traditionalists who denounced this practice as mere "gyrations." "The very fact that college bands throughout the country have copied our maneuvers shows how favorably they have been considered in sections of the country outside of our own little eastern cozy-corner," Ad countered. "May I venture to add that some of these bands are among the finest in the country?"[2]

Upon his graduation from Harvard, Ad traveled to Europe for "study," like John Dickson Carr spending considerable time in London and Paris, where he learned jiu-jitsu and organized a dance orchestra which performed at Ostend, Belgium and London's Four Hundred Club ("the most amusing place," confided *The Gourmet's Guide to London*, "to keep awake after all the restaurants are shut"). After returning to the United States he finally got around to attending law school, from which he graduated in 1928. Upon his graduation, however, he asked himself "Who wants to be a lawyer?" and embarked instead upon a career in fiction writing. By 1934, when at the age of 32 he wed Berenice "Bunny" Levin—the pretty, button-black-eyed, 24-year-old youngest child of Sam Levin, a prosperous Fall River, Massachusetts, grocer of Lithuanian origin—Ad had published short stories in the prominent Canadian magazine *Maclean's*. After their marriage the couple settled in Brookline, a town adjacent to Boston where the Kennedy family had resided in the 1910s and 1920s, and Ad began writing his first detective novel, *Death on the Campus*. The next year publisher Thomas Y. Crowell of New York published *Death on the Campus*, along with another mystery which has been reissued by Coachwhip, New Hampshire native Kenneth Whipple's *The Fires at Fitch's Folly*. Ad dedicated the novel to his wife, mother, and brother Arthur.

When Bunny Levin Simmons was growing up, the Levins of
Fall River had resided at 298 Third Street, a mere stroll of two
minutes from the house where Andrew and Abby Borden, father
and stepmother of Lizzie and Emma Borden, were bloodily and
infamously murdered with a hatchet on August 4, 1892. At the
time when the Levins lived at 298 Third Street, Lizzie Borden of
"forty whacks" infamy, who had been tried and acquitted of the
horrific murders, lived about a mile away at a much more fash-
ionable home, Maplecroft, where she died in 1927, when Bunny
Levin was 17. Among Bunny's siblings at 298 Third Street was
Isadore "Izzy" Levin, a rising young lawyer who at the time of
Ad and Bunny's nuptials had already argued a case of corporate
law before the United States Supreme Court, to the approbation
of Justice Louis Brandeis, who approvingly wrote future Supreme
Court Justice Felix Frankfurter that Isadore had "made a most
creditable appearance in our Court—well prepared, dignified,
tactful. With experience added, he should do much."

THE LEVIN FAMILY HOME IN FALL RIVER, MASSACHUSETTS
(PHOTO BY CURT EVANS)

Although I have found no word from Justice Brandies concerning Ad's *Death on the Campus* (we know that near the end of his life Oliver Wendell Holmes, Jr. praised Rex Stout's 1934 detective novel *Fer de Lance*, in which the famous sleuthing team of Nero Wolfe and Archie Goodwin made its debut), the novel was greeted with favorable notices in American newspapers. One particularly creative reviewer, Paul Allen of the *Brooklyn Daily Eagle*, gave his favorable account of the novel in an eight-stanza poem, in a column titled "The Verse Side of Crime":

Professor Ingram, on his way
To Chatham House one fatal day,
Saw things that were a bit askew—
More so, indeed, than then he knew;
    Since English was his specialty,
    He hadn't studied mystery.

So when a chap he'd had in class
From Chatham House was seen to pass,
Ben Ingram's subtle mind was not
Attuned to guess a murder plot;
    And placidly he kept his route,
    Not knowing there was death about.

Inside and on his desk Ben found
A note, as he was fussing round;
It read: "Come up when you arrive,"
(Signed) "Yerkes," who then was not alive;
    For someone else had called on Yerkes
    And then had given him the works.

It certainly made Ingram hot
To find his friend completely shot!
No more would Yerkes and Ingram romp
In pleasant fields of English comp;
    And not a doubt existed that
    The killer was a dirty rat.

Then Ingram called up Prexy Meade,
Who found him upset, indeed,
To realize some bungling fool
Had killed a man right in his school:
>    "Ye gods, what will the people say!"
>    This thought drove him almost distrait.

Policemen came and found that they
Were not considered quite *au fait*,
For Prexy Meade kept telling how
The news must not be published now;
>    And Ingram knowing more than less,
>    Just let the bluecoats guess and guess.

Two members of the faculty
He'd seen slink off from tree to tree;
He'd mentioned neither act nor name,
For one was daddy of his flame—
>    And in the end he simply had
>    To solve the crime to save her dad.

This tale we highly recommend,
It's sure to hold you to the end.
And though it springs a sharp surprise,
"Why not?" you'll say; "It satisfies."

Literally more prosaically, Isaac Anderson of the *New York Times Book Review* pronounced that *Death on the Campus* had "excitement and bafflement galore," while Dorothy Barnes of the Austin *Daily Texan* assured her readers that they would find themselves reading the book at one sitting "because you will be curious enough to ascertain your deductions concerning the identity of the murderer." Particularly amusing is the notice of the novel in the *LA Times*, wherein the reviewer declares that Ad's mystery is "fast enough for any fan," adding: "From the moment Prof. Ingram . . . finds the dead body of Prof. Yerkes, one terror follows rapidly on the heels of another. . . . if you ever thought that college professors are slow and timid, you'll be converted to a new idea."

My copy of *Death on the Campus* is inscribed by Ad to his "good friends and staunch supporters," Bertha and Nettie Trustman, the unmarried daughters of Boston dentist Israel Trustman and his wife Pessie Rubin, who, like Ad and Bunny's parents, were immigrant Russian Jews. The Trustmans settled in the Boston's West End at 59 Chambers Street, making them immediate neighbors of the late actor Leonard Nimoy, whose family lived in a tenement at 87 Chambers Street. Formerly a schoolteacher, Nettie by the time of the publication of *Death on the Campus* had become, according to her nephew, attorney and film screenwriter Alan Trustman (among his credits are *The Thomas Crowne Affair*,

INSCRIPTION BY ADDISON SIMMONS
(CURT EVANS COLLECTION)

*They Call Me Mr. Tibbs!,* and *Bullitt*), secretary to the Brookline chief of police "and the only Jew working in the Town Hall."

Not long after the publication of *Death on the Campus,* Ad and Bunny left Brookline for Hollywood, where Ad scripted radio plays for *Hollywood Hotel* and the screenplay for its 1937 film musical version (working with Wyllis Cooper, creator of *Lights Out* and *Quiet, Please*), and later Chicago, where he worked on *The First Nighter Program* and *Grand Hotel,* both of which were sponsored by The Campana Company, a large cosmetics business head-quartered in Batavia, Illinois, and *The Wayside Theater,* sponsored by the Chicago Motor Club. Among Ad's many radio scripts are a number which most definitely are of the crime and mystery genre, including *Dark Dilemma, Three Who Face Death, Bullets in the Night, The Desperate Remedy, Men Don't So Such Things, Six Months to Live, In the Dark, In the Jury's Hands, One Night at the Black Dog* and *Vengeance is Mine* (apologies to Mickey Spillane). The description of *Dark Dilemma* in the *Daily Iowan's* "Tuning In" column suggests that Ad had not forgotten his family's im-migrant origins:

> *The original story centers around co-stars Barbara Luddy, as the girl accused of murdering her vindictive stepfather, and Les Tremayne, as the bum who aban-dons his freight train touring long enough to discover the murder and the murderer. A strong supporting role is played by Michael Romano as Stilette, Les' Italian hobo companion.*[3]

Ad drew on his experience writing for radio when in 1946 he published his second and final detective novel, *Dead Weight,* which was published by Phoenix Press. More than a decade had elapsed since the publication of his last mystery novel, and Ad's writing style had significantly changed since then, becoming much more individualized. *Death on the Campus* was very much a first mystery novel, playing it safe with more of a by the numbers approach (aside from the extravagant dénouement), while *Dead Weight* was exuberant and snappy in writing style and baroque in plot, throwing in, as the *Saturday Review* put it, "everything but sound effects." In the *San Francisco Chronicle* Anthony Boucher for his part pronounced that the novel had "quite a bit of ingenuity."

One might have thought this sufficient encouragement for the 44-year-old author to continue penning crime novels, but perhaps the radio biz, a demanding mistress, sapped Ad's energy for other creative writing efforts. Ad Simmons died in 1972 at the age of 70, apparently without having published another novel in his last 25 years of life. An exploration of his radio mysteries might bear some further interesting fruit for vintage crime fiction fans, however.

### *Death on the Campus* (1935)

While American mystery writers during the Golden Age of detective fiction seem to have lacked the enthusiasm of their English contemporaries for committing murders at primary schools (though there was Stuart Palmer's *Murder on the Black-board*, 1932, with that indefatigable schoolteacher and snoop

Giving the go-ahead signal in "Hollywood Hotel's" control-room are (left to right): Addison Simmons, staff writer; Diana Bourbon, associate producer; and F. G. Ibbett, the show's producer and director. Standing in the doorway is Onlooker Maury Wood, formerly of Chicago's WGN direction staff

FROM *RADIO GUIDE* (JAN. 29, 1938)

Hildegarde Withers), they do seem to have enjoyed bumping off teachers and students in colleges, publishing such puzzlers as, for example, Clifford Orr's *The Dartmouth Murders* (1929), John Stephen Strange's *Murder on the Ten Yard Line* (1931), Milton Propper's *The Student Fraternity Murder*, Whitman Chambers' *The Campanile Murders* (1933), Kathleen Sproul's *Death and the Professors* (1933), Addison Simmons's *Death on the Campus* (1935), Joel Y. Dane's *Murder Cum Laude* (1935), Kurt Steel's *Murder Goes to College* (1936), Timothy Fuller's *Harvard Has a Homicide* (1936), and John Miller's *Murder of a Professor* (1937). Addison Simmons's university setting in his novel remains rather anonymous throughout, although the desperately scandal-averse president is a portrait which people should still recognize, sadly today. The dénouement is unexpectedly and rather fantastically violent, yet keen clue fanciers should discern a pleasing trail of clues to follow though the author's maze of mystery, alongside English professor Ben Ingram, who hopes desperately to exonerate from suspicion of murder noted Shakespeare scholar John Hardwick Bailey, father of his winsome sweetheart, Mary.

To me the greatest weakness in the novel, particularly at a time when the female readership of mysteries was markedly expanding, is its lack of any interesting women characters. Women exist in the novel only as highly idealized wives and sweethearts of rather stolid males, as well as a few nondescript housekeepers and one bad girl type, regrettably glimpsed only fleetingly. Having lived more of life within the intervening decade, Ad would evince a stronger grip on the portrayal of the daughters of Eve in his second mystery.

### *Dead Weight* (1946)

In *Dead Weight*, which Ad Simmons dedicated to his beloved wife Bunny, Chicago radio scripters Ed MacIntyre and Walt Tuttle, authors of the hugely popular serial melodrama *Home Town*, decide to quit the grueling radio biz and settle, along with Ed's wife Binnie, in Walt's own home town of Hamsted (probably located in Massachusetts, not very far from Ad's Boston), where they plan to run a pharmacy. "Maybe the hydrochloric would go away and mind its own business and nobody would have to think about nervous breakdowns lurking around the corner," thinks Ed hopefully of their plan; yet almost immediately after their move to Hamsted Ed and Binnie find themselves plunged into a real life case of murder, when Walt is found shot dead in a stall at the pharmacy, a scrap of paper clutched in his hand and a glass of strawberry ice cream soda overturned before him.

So who whacked Walt at the pharmacy? Could it have been someone from Walt's and Ed's old Chicago life, like histrionic radio account executive Harry Leibowitz, imperious radio sponsor Slade Latimer ("one of the wealthiest men in the country") or Latimer's sexy, hot-blooded daughter Sandra, who still carried—rather fiercely—a torch for Walt? Or could the murderer be a local candidate? What does the town simpleton, the strawberry soda guzzling "Dodo" Brown, know about the crime? And is he really as simple as he appears? Ed and Binnie find themselves trapped in a real-life mystery melodrama as strange as anything Ed and Walt ever concocted for *Home Town*—one that puts them in peril of their own lives! Readers who see in Ed and Binnie portraits of Ad and Bunny may just be on to something, but can they beat the fictional couple to the identity of the murderer?

## Endnotes

[1] "To Play in Worcester," *Harvard Crimson*, 23 April 1923.

[2] "In Defense of the Band," *Harvard Crimson*, 31 October 1923.

[3] Les Tremayne (1913-2003), who replaced Don Ameche on *The First Nighter Program* in 1936, was one of the most prominent America radio performers.

# DEATH ON THE CAMPUS

FOR BUNNY, MOTHER AND ARTHUR

". . . There is no den in the wide world to hide a rogue. There is no such thing as concealment. Commit a crime and the earth is made of glass. Commit a crime and it seems as if a coat of snow fell on the ground, such as reveals in the woods the track of every partridge, and fox and squirrel and mole. You cannot recall the spoken word, you cannot wipe out the foot-track, you cannot draw up the ladder, so as to leave no inlet or clew. Always some damning circumstance transpires. The laws and substances of nature, water, snow, wind, gravitation, become penalties. . . ."

Ralph Waldo Emerson: *Compensation*

# 1
## WEDNESDAY 3 P.M.

At three o'clock Professor Ben Ingram left his home and set off at a leisurely pace for Chatham House.

Ben Ingram's home was three blocks west of the campus on quiet Elm Street. It was a rambling old house, with an added ell at the rear. It had stood many years, and here Ben Ingram had been born thirty-five years before. Here his illustrious father, David Ingram, Chadwick Professor of English in the university, had lived and died.

Ben Ingram had grown to a size befitting a large house. He stood to a height of six feet two and across his chest he was broad as his height needed. He had an easy stride as he walked; and his handsome face, forceful yet kindly, told of his preoccupation as he moved along.

He went east across the campus. It was a warm late fall day. Students wandered here and there, entering and leaving dormitories and the library. Professor Ingram met several students and spoke a word to those whom he knew, and came at length to the east end of the campus.

He went through the gate here, strolled across the narrow road that separated the campus proper and East Park. East Park ran north and south, the length of the campus on this side, and at the northern end it turned westward and went along the north side of the campus, there being called North Park. It was a narrow park with benches and shade trees. On warm days students sometimes sat in the shade of the trees and studied, and at night they came here and sat in the moonlight and the place was sometimes called Lovers' Lane.

Just as he entered the park, Ingram glanced up and looked ahead to Chatham House and saw someone come out. It was a student—Luciano was his name, Ingram knew—Guido Luciano. He had been a member of Ingram's Junior English class the year before, but was not taking any of his courses this year.

Luciano came down the small lane from Chatham House to Paisley Road, which separated East Park from the lane itself. His step was quicker than Ingram's. They met halfway across the park. Ingram, who had momentarily again fallen into preoccupation, glanced at Luciano. The student spoke a soft good afternoon, and Ingram nodded in reply.

He was a thin, smooth-looking youth, this Luciano; older, it seemed, than the average university senior. Those dark eyes of his had probably seen much life. Veiled, confident eyes.

The professor emerged from the park, crossed Paisley Road and strolled down Chatham Lane to the front door of Chatham House.

In Chatham House the English department had its conference quarters. Here the professors had their offices and met students for periodic discussions of their work. It was a long, two-story building, wooden, painted a canary yellow, with green shutters. It had a basement in which the janitor, Schultz, a campus character, lived.

The front door, facing south, was in the exact middle of the building, whose length was at right angles to Paisley Road. Three worn wooden steps led into a small vestibule, beyond which was the corridor that ran the length of the building. The stairway to the upper floor was at the left in the corridor as one entered from the vestibule.

Ingram went into the building, crossed the vestibule, went to the right down the corridor, to the second room on his left there. He opened the door with his key and stepped over the threshold.

He closed the door behind him. It was a small office, and the professor seemed gigantic in it. There was a desk that stood before the window and an old swivel chair, so placed that when the professor seated himself there to work, the window was at his right. There were two other chairs, one of which bore an aged typewriter. There was a small bookcase and a green metal filing case.

Ingram dropped his hat on the desk and sat down in the swivel chair. He opened a desk drawer and took out a rough briar pipe and a tin humidor of tobacco. Leaning back in the chair he filled his pipe and, as he did so, glanced out the window.

Behind the building was a thicket of brush and grass, tall enough to reach to a man's waist or higher. Out there was a path but it was seldom used. Probably Schultz the janitor was the only one who traversed it.

Ingram returned his attention to his pipe, and it was out of the corner of his eye that he saw the two figures move out there in the brush. They were perhaps twenty yards from the rear of the building and they had stepped out from behind a small group of trees in the center of the area. Ingram turned his head to look out again, and his brow wrinkled in slow puzzlement. He stared.

Why anyone at all should be walking out there was strange enough. But why the dignified Professors Bailey and Davis should be out there was more than Ingram could understand. Bailey was in the lead, and a few yards behind him the tall Davis hastened. Their heads were bent low as if in an effort at concealment.

Bailey and Davis were members of the English department. Bailey was John Hardwick Bailey, recognized as one of the foremost students of Shakespeare. Davis was Thaddeus Davis, authority on English poetry.

Ben Ingram stood up as these two passed from sight behind another group of trees. From this point out to the road they were hidden from his view. He had another glimpse of them as they reached the road, as they went hurrying away in the northerly direction. They did not, oddly enough, walk side by side. The longer legs of Davis now carried him on ahead of Bailey, though Bailey hastened along at full stride.

They went out of sight down the road as Ingram stood watching. He turned away at length; then, hearing a step in the corridor, he went to the door, opened it and glanced out.

Just at the moment he opened, he heard the hasty closing of another door. It was to the right, far down the corridor, he thought, but he could not determine which door it was. Down there, besides the private offices of other professors, were two rooms usually left unlocked, rooms used for examinations and as study rooms for the students.

Ingram stepped out into the corridor, stood silent and listened. He was certain that that door, whichever it was, had closed because he had opened his.

And it was at this moment that he sensed definitely the fact that something was wrong here. He was unable to understand it. He remained for a moment in the doorway, then went back to his desk, leaving the door open now.

He picked up his pipe, which he had laid on the desk on his way to the door. It had gone dead. He struck a match and lighted it again, puffing slowly, thoughtfully, listening carefully. Then, standing beside the desk, he shrugged slightly and went to the typewriter on the chair in the corner.

He picked up the machine, set it on his desk and sat down before it. From a pocket he took out several sheets of yellow typewriter paper and laid them on the desk beside the machine. They bore closely penciled notes for the second chapter of the book he was writing: *The Development of the English Novel.*

He slipped a sheet of paper into the machine and sat before it, staring at the keyboard. It was only then that he noticed a small folded slip of paper on the floor near the door.

He got up, picked up the paper. It was a note. It had been written with the blue-gray lead of an indelible pencil. It read: "*Dear Ben: Please come upstairs and see me when you get in. I'll be here all afternoon. Something important.*" It was signed: "*Yerkes.*" Below all this, at the left, was written: "*1:30.*"

Ingram slipped the note into his pocket and stepped out of the office, unlatching the door before he closed it. He started across the corridor towards the stairway.

Reaching the second floor, he went down towards the west end of the corridor. Professor Yerkes's office was second from the end, on the left, his windows looking down into the lane at the front of the building.

Yerkes was a few years older than Ingram, just short of forty; a tall, thin serious man; a man with a shrewd, acute brain. His specialty was English composition. His hobby was investigating the strange little mysteries that came up now and then in the university. He had solved, on one occasion, the strange case of a kleptomaniac; on another, the surreptitious leaking out of advance information on examination questions, and at other times, problems of a like nature. He was gifted at this, his form of relaxation.

Ingram reached Yerkes's door and knocked. There was no reply. "Yerkes!" he called. "Philip!"

There was no reply. Ingram glanced at his wrist watch. It was twenty past three. Yerkes had said he would be there all afternoon. Usually he meant what he said. If he had had to go out, he would have left another note explaining.

Ingram tried the door. It was locked. He turned away from it, went down to the west end of the corridor and stood at the window there, looking down into Paisley Road and saw, at this moment, a student emerging from the lane into Paisley Road.

The youth, a pale, blond lad, was moving swiftly, and he glanced back with a furtiveness that made Ingram think of Bailey and Davis in the thicket at the rear. The student was hurrying, hurrying not to something but away from something. On impulse, Ingram went swiftly back to Yerkes's door. The feeling that something was wrong seized him now like a gigantic, powerful hand.

"Yerkes!" he called. "Philip Yerkes! Are you in there?"

Then he went suddenly down on one knee and looked through the keyhole of the lower, unused lock. The next moment he stood up, stepped back and drove his foot through the thin door panel. Then he reached in, released the snap-lock inside and swung open the door.

Professor Yerkes sat in the chair at his desk, back to the door. He had fallen forward on to the desk, one arm under his head, the other hanging limply down, the tips of the long, thin fingers touching the floor.

Ingram was beside him at a single stride.

"Yerkes!" he cried. "Yerkes, old man! What's the trouble?" And stood horrified as he saw the deepening crimson stain on Yerkes's chest.

He put no hand upon Yerkes. That he was dead he had no reason to doubt. He stood frozen beside him, stunned, knowing, in the full minute of shock that followed, nothing but the single fact that Yerkes was dead, murdered. He fought away the stupefying weight that held him motionless; tried to master another thought besides this one that froze him so. He stood beside Philip Yerkes and stared at him, at the dark hair with its flecks of gray, at the sleeping face whose profile was white and strained in death.

He emerged from his bewilderment like a man finding his way through a heavy fog to its edges. He went slowly to the telephone at the other end of Yerkes's desk, picked it up and said to the instant voice of the operator: "Get me President Meade at once. Urgent. This is Professor Ingram."

He had to wait for half a minute and then came the throaty voice of Dr. Meade. "Yes, professor? Something urgent?"

"Yes, urgent," Ingram replied. "Something that requires your presence at once at Chatham House."

"But, professor, I am busy at the moment—"

"I can't explain over the phone, doctor," Ingram interrupted, "but it's something that comes before anything else, no matter how important."

There was a brief silence on the wire. Then Dr. Meade said: "Very well, professor. I'll come right over." He hung up.

Ingram signaled for the operator once more. "Get me Dr. Royal," he said, and shortly Dr. Royal was on the wire.

"Something's happened here at Chatham House," Ingram told him. "Can't tell you over the phone. I wish you'd come over at once. Better bring your bag."

"What is it?" Dr. Royal demanded. "Why are you so dark about it?"

"I'll tell you when you get here. Hurry, please, won't you?"

"Five minutes," said the doctor, and rang off.

For a brief time Ingram stared dumbly at Yerkes's body. Then he went slowly out of the office, closed the door and went downstairs, thoughts crowding in upon him now.

Bailey and Davis. His father's staunchest friends. Bailey, in the bad market many years ago, had saved his father from disaster. Davis had given his very life's blood once, long ago too, to save his father from death. The three had gone to college together, had roomed together. They had been as blood-kin to Ben himself. They had been good to him when he was a child; had been as boisterous children with him. He had grown up under their eyes. They had showered him with gifts all his life. They loved him as they loved their own. Grown to manhood he had hunted with them, fished with them, studied, debated with them. From them he had obtained wisdom; with them he had had enormous good fun. And was this the end—that he should tell of seeing them there under circumstances suspicious enough for police to tie them up to this murder—even pin it directly on them? And there was Mary Bailey, whom he loved. . . .

He went into his own office, sat down, then got up again and walked the floor. He gathered up his papers and put them into his pocket. He went out into the corridor, to see that no one should enter and go upstairs to—that. He paced the length of the corridor, down towards the study rooms, down there where, shortly before, he had heard the surreptitious closing of a door and, as he had thought, footsteps.

Before the door of the last study room he halted, facing it. Then he opened it, thrust it wide and remained outside looking in, his gaze, aimless, wandering slowly from corner to corner of the room.

There was a small brown notebook on the first chair in the second row. The chairs were a combination chair-and-desk, like lunchroom chairs with a single, broad, table-like arm. On one of these arms lay the notebook.

Ingram went in and picked it up. There was a bare chance that the one who had prowled here had left it. He regretted now that he had not gone down the corridor in the first place to see who was there. It might have cleared up this matter. But if it had been the killer, that killer might have used another bullet. . . .

He opened the notebook. The name on the inside cover was "Leonard Crane." And Ingram recalled now the blond student who had fled out of Chatham Lane, recalled too that his name was Crane. He put the notebook into his pocket and went out into the corridor once more.

He was standing there when President Meade arrived with Dr. Royal. The president was a short, stout man, gray, red of face, with hard blue eyes that never told what he was thinking. He came in brusquely and Dr. Royal was behind him. Royal was tall and fat, double-chinned, cheerful-faced. He was the chief university physician.

"Well, professor," the president began sharply, "what's happened? I hope it's no fool's errand."

"It isn't," Ingram said briefly. "It's—it's murder."

"Murder!" the president cried. "Murder? Who was murdered? And by whom?"

Dr. Royal closed the door behind him and stood silent just over the threshold of the vestibule, waiting for Professor Ingram to answer these questions.

"It's Philip Yerkes," Ingram said. "Upstairs, in his office. I don't know who did it. I found him there, dead."

President Meade started directly for the stairway. Dr. Royal's gaze met Ingram's quizzically. Then the doctor started up behind President Meade, Ingram following. At the head of the stairs Meade stopped, turned.

"Have you notified the police?" he asked Ingram.

Ingram shook his head.

"Not yet," he said. "I thought—well, I thought you ought to know about it first."

Meade nodded brusquely. "Quite right," he replied. "Quite right." He went on to Professor Yerkes's office. At the door he stopped again and stared at the broken panel.

"I smashed the door," Ingram explained.

Ingram put his hand through the break in the panel and released the lock, opened the door and walked in. He said nothing, but stood there and glanced back at Dr. Royal. The doctor entered, set down his bag. Then he bent over the body and, without disturbing its position, made a brief examination.

"Bullet," he said, standing up. "Better call the police."

Meade asked: "Has he been dead long?"

"He's still warm," the doctor said.

Meade pulled thoughtfully at his lip, then turned to Ingram. "What do you know about this," he asked, "besides what you've told us?"

"Nothing," Ingram answered. "I came to the building at a little after three. There was a note under my door from—him, asking me to come upstairs and see him when I got here. I came up, broke in the door—and found him."

"How'd you happen to break in the door?"

Ingram frowned. "I'd better give you my impressions from the beginning," he said. "Then you'll understand. When I entered the building it was all quiet here. I went into my office and was sitting there when I heard footsteps in the corridor. When I opened to look out, no one was there and the footsteps had ceased, but I thought that a door had closed down at the west end just as I opened mine. I didn't think to investigate. I left my door open. It was then that I found the note—in my office, on the floor. I simply hadn't seen it before. I came upstairs, knocked, got no answer, sensed that something was wrong and looked through the keyhole." President Meade sniffed. "I saw him there and called to him. Then I broke in the panel. I phoned you at once."

"You say you saw no one in the building?"

"No one."

"Did you meet any one on your way over here—near here?"

"Yes. A student. Luciano is his name, I believe. As I walked into East Park from the campus I saw him come out of this building. We passed in East Park. And then, just before I broke down this door, I saw another student—I believe his name is Crane— saw him come out of Chatham Lane. I saw him from the west window of the corridor."

"He might just have been going by the building, through the lane, might he not?" Meade asked.

"Yes," Ingram agreed. "But there's another thing. Just before you came, I found this notebook in the furthest study room downstairs. It's Crane's."

President Meade took the notebook and glanced through it briefly, then slipped it into his pocket.

"You didn't hear a shot on your way over, did you?" he asked.

"No."

Meade frowned. Yerkes's death was regrettable enough, but the evil publicity that the university would get was his chief concern. He was figuring that if it was possible for themselves to lay hands quickly on the murderer and turn him over to the police, the affair would be only a single episode, not a prolonged police investigation with reporters and camera men dragging the university into the press day in and day out. The papers were always greedy for university scandal. It had always been the policy of the university to discourage publicity as much as possible.

"I want to speak with Crane and Luciano at once," he said. "Will you be good enough, professor, to have them located immediately and sent here? In the meantime we'll lock this room again. We'll go downstairs to your office, professor."

They went out into the corridor and Dr. Royal closed the door. Ingram started down the stairs and the others came behind him. At the foot of the stairs, Ingram took out his handkerchief and mopped his brow where heavy perspiration had broken forth despite the fact that the place was not overwarm.

It was the thought of Professors Bailey and Davis that disturbed him so. So far he had not mentioned them.

And he never would. Though heaven should fall, he never would.

# 3
## WEDNESDAY 3:45 P.M.

Behind him President Meade was muttering in a subdued but savage undertone, his habit when troubles preyed upon his mind. Dr. Royal was silent. The two followed Ingram into his office and sat down, President Meade in a chair, Dr. Royal on a corner of the desk, while Ingram telephoned. While he waited, Meade took out a long cigar, bit off the end and lighted up, annoyance in his every gesture.

Ingram spoke with the dean's office and asked to have Luciano and Crane located at once and sent over to Chatham House. When he hung up, President Meade was staring at him through a cloud of smoke.

Meade said: "I want to see that note—from Yerkes."

Ingram handed it over. The president read it, turned it over, handed it back.

"What did he want to see you about that was so important?" the president asked. "Do you know?"

Ingram shook his head. "I haven't any idea. Twice before he's done just this, though—left a note saying he had something important—"

"And on those occasions it was—?"

"Well," Ingram declared thoughtfully, "it had to do with his investigating hobby. On those two occasions he wanted to tell me what he had discovered; wanted to ask my opinion. I was thinking that perhaps he had another such problem—and an answer to it."

"You mean matters like that of Hooper the kleptomaniac and—?"

"Exactly."

"What problem had he been investigating lately?" Dr. Royal put in.

Ingrain said thoughtfully: "I don't know. The only thing I can think of is Professor Coombs's death. Just after Coombs died, Yerkes went around in a kind of nervous agitation for days."

"You mean," Meade put in, "that he didn't believe Coombs shot himself? Certainly the police were satisfied. And you were, weren't you, doctor?"

Dr. Royal nodded.

"If Yerkes had suspected anything, anything that was hidden," Meade went on, "he'd have reported the matter to the authorities, wouldn't he?"

"No," Ingram replied. "I'm quite sure he wouldn't have done that. When he was investigating on his own, he never went to the police until he had something definite—a solution—to offer. If he failed—as I think he must have more than once—he never said anything about it to anyone. None of us knew, for instance, that he was working on the Hooper case. He told no one until he had solved it."

"Hm. . . . But you're only shooting in the dark, professor— about Coombs. I dare say any number of us were as much in a state of agitation after his death as Yerkes."

"I have a little more to go on," Ingram declared. "I had a chat with Yerkes after Coombs's death. He said he was almost certain Coombs wasn't the type of man to resort to suicide."

"He'd just lost his daughter," Meade argued. "He was overworked, upset. The police were satisfied that was sufficient to cause suicide."

"Yerkes didn't always agree with the police."

President Meade's cigar had gone out. He looked at its gray end reflectively and went on: "Then what you are intimating, professor, is that Yerkes had learned that Coombs had been murdered, that he had discovered the murderer and that the murderer killed Yerkes to keep his secret dark. Is that it?"

Ingram nodded slowly. "That's what I think," he said.

The president got up and began to walk up and down in the small office. The door was open to the corridor and he stepped out and glanced from right to left, looking and listening intently. He turned about, stepped into the office again and inquired:

"Are you sure there's no one else in the building?"

"I'm not positive," Ingram replied, "but I've seen no one and heard no one."

The president declared: "We've got to find out. We must look in the locked offices. Where's the janitor? He'll have a pass key. Schultz. He has rooms downstairs. Perhaps he's down there now."

"I'll go and look for him if you like," Ingram offered.

"Do, please," Meade urged, and Ingram went out.

At the east end of the corridor, a narrow, dark stairway descended to the basement. With a hand on the banister, Ingram went down and the stairs creaked under his great weight. He came down into a stone-walled corridor, whitewashed but now gray, and lighted with only a dim bulb at the far end over the door to the janitor's quarters. Past a line of barrels, empty and neatly arrayed, Ingram went. The ceiling was close overhead. There was a musty cellar smell and the echoing of his footsteps ahead and behind. On the right was the rear wall of the building—the north wall. On the left were wooden-fronted bins with padlocked doors; storage places for desks and chairs and the like.

Ingram came to the janitor's door and knocked. The knock went down the corridor behind him and came back again. But when that sound died, no other sound came, no answer from within the janitor's quarters. Ingram knocked again. Then he laid a hand on the doorknob and tried it. It merely rattled in his hand. The door was locked.

He waited a few moments longer, then turned away and went back along the corridor, up the stairs and to his office. The president was staring out the window and faced about quickly as Ingram entered.

"He's not there," Ingram said. "I got no answer."

"At his duties, probably," the president said; and Dr. Royal snapped his fingers softly in recollection.

"I think not," he said. "Don't know why I didn't think of it till now, but Schultz came over to my office yesterday and saw Dr. Harper. Harper said he had grippe and told him to go up to the infirmary. That's where he is now, I suppose."

President Meade sat down at the telephone and asked for the head janitor's office.

"Who is doing Janitor Schultz's work while he's at the infirmary?" he asked.

He listened for a few moments, then hung up. He glanced then from Professor Ingram to Dr. Royal. "He didn't apply for relief," he said.

Then he rang the infirmary. "This is President Meade. Is Janitor Schultz there—ill with the grippe?" He listened, waited, listened again, spoke his thanks and hung up.

"He isn't there," he stated. "He hasn't been there."

"That's odd," Dr. Royal said. "What do you suppose happened?"

"Your guess is as good as mine," Meade shrugged.

The front door of Chatham House opened. Some one came into the vestibule and then into the corridor. Ingram looked out. It was Luciano.

"Come in, Luciano," Ingram called.

The dark Italian youth came across the corridor. He was hatless and his smooth dark hair reflected the light from the large window over the corridor entrance. It was like light on dark water.

He reached the doorway, looked from one to another of these men, nodded respectfully to President Meade and asked: "I'm wanted here?"

"Yes," said Meade. "Come in. Sit down there."

The president, seated at Ingram's desk, motioned to the chair across from him. Dr. Royal seated himself on the desk again. Ingram stood by the door.

"Luciano," the president began, "at about three o'clock, or a little later, this afternoon, Professor Ingram met you crossing East Park, going towards the campus. Will you be good enough to tell us where you had been just before the professor saw you—where you were coming from?"

Luciano's brow went up a little in surprise.

"Why," he said with a soft smile, "I'd been out for a walk and I came by Chatham House here and stopped in for a moment to drop a paper into Professor Bailey's theme box. I was coming directly from here when I met the professor." He shifted his glance for a second to Ingram, then back to President Meade.

"How long were you here in the building?" Meade asked.

"Not more than a minute or so. I had the theme in my pocket. I took it out, glanced over it, then dropped it into the box."

"And then?"

"Then I went out, up the path and over to the park where I met Professor Ingram, then back to my rooms."

"Did you see or hear any one in the building while you were here?"

Luciano reflected. "I didn't see anyone, but I heard voices upstairs."

"Ah! Voices that you recognized?"

"Not all of them. I think I recognized Professor Yerkes's voice. It's peculiar, sharp, penetrating. The others I didn't recognize." He wore a puzzled look now, and glanced from one to another of the university officials.

"How many other voices?" Meade asked.

"Two, I think. I can't be sure."

"Did it sound as if they were quarreling?"

"No, sir, it didn't. They weren't loud enough to tell, I suppose."

"Could you tell from which room—or at least from which direction they came?"

Luciano shook his head. "Not which room, but I think they came from that end of the building." He indicated the west end, in the direction of Yerkes's office.

"You didn't hear any strange sound—a cry or—a shot?"

Luciano's brow went up sharply. "A shot? No, sir. I didn't hear anything like that. And no cry. Was somebody hurt?"

The president tapped the desk thoughtfully. "You'll know in good time," he said.

At this moment the telephone rang. Ingram reached for the instrument and answered. It was the dean's office, reporting

delay in locating Crane. He had not been in his room but had
been found in the library and was on his way to Chatham House
now. Ingram repeated this message to President Meade. The president nodded, then said to Luciano:

"That'll be all for the present. You may go. I must ask you,
however, to make no mention of this—any of it—to anyone. In
due time the whole matter will become public."

"Yes, sir." Luciano got up and went out. Ingram met his eyes
as he passed him at the door. Those eyes were clouded with a
frown. Luciano went out of the building.

"Well," Meade grumbled, "what do you think?"

Dr. Royal shrugged. "Sounded innocent enough."

There was a silence in the office for a few minutes now. It
was broken when the president pushed back his chair, got up and
stood at the window. He remained there for a short time, looking
out into the thicket of grass and bushes where Ingram had seen
Professors Bailey and Davis. Ingram's eyes wandered to the spot
where he had first espied these two, the group of trees in the
center of the area there. Something urged him now to speak out
that he had seen them, that he had seen them going away in a
manner that was suspicious. Something kept saying to him: "You
told of Luciano. You told of Crane. Now tell of these two. Tell
of them. It is your duty. It is something you must do. You must
not shield them."

But something else laid a hand upon his lips and kept him
silent.

He seated himself, hands in his pockets, great shoulders
hunched, staring out the window and saying to himself:

"No one knows that I saw them. No one can know. Had I not
turned my head to look through that window, I should not have
seen them. Very well. I did not turn my head. I did not see them.
Right or wrong, I did not see them."

This was indeed his dark hour.

# 4
## WEDNESDAY 4:10 P.M.

There was a click and the outer door opened. The blond student came into the corridor and halted there, looking across towards Ingram's office. President Meade stood scowling at him.

Crane came forward hesitantly. He halted again, moistened dry lips slowly and said:

"They sent me word from the dean's office that I was wanted here. I'm Leonard Crane."

"Come in," Meade said. He sat down again at Ingram's desk. Crane entered and stood before him. Meade did not offer him a seat. Ingram, from his corner, studied the youth's face carefully. It was pale, sallow, the features thin and tired-looking. His shoulders were stooped and narrow. His hands moved nervously and the look in his eyes was one of awe if not fear.

Abruptly, tactlessly, Ingram thought, President Meade plunged directly into the heart of the matter.

"Crane," he said, "I want you to tell me what you know about the death of Professor Yerkes."

There was a sharp, short intake of breath by Crane. His eyes were suddenly frightened and staring.

"I—I don't know anything—about the—the death of Professor Yerkes," he said. "I didn't know he was dead. I didn't know anything about it at all."

"Did you know that anything had happened to him?" Meade demanded.

"No, sir, I didn't."

"But you were in the building here less than an hour ago—you'll admit that, won't you?"

Crane swallowed with an effort. He shook his head.

"No, sir. I wasn't here in the building. I haven't been here all day—till now."

"Suppose I tell you that you were seen here!" the president snapped, leaning forward and glaring at Crane.

"No, sir," Crane insisted. "I wasn't here. No one saw me here. I haven't been here today."

The president reached into his pocket and took out Crane's small brown notebook and laid it on the desk. Crane stared at it fearfully.

Meade said: "Young man, there's no use in lying to me. You were seen leaving here. You were seen in the lane downstairs—by Professor Ingram. And this—this notebook—was found in the study room at the other end of the corridor here. Do you still deny that you were here?"

"Yes, sir," Crane retorted. "I say I wasn't here. I don't know anything about the death of Professor Yerkes. I didn't even know he was dead until you told me!"

"Then what are you getting so excited about?"

Crane was trembling violently now. "Because," he said, "you're trying to get me to admit I killed Professor Yerkes."

"I didn't say he was killed, young man," Meade said glibly. "I merely spoke of his death. How do you know he was killed? Come now, speak up!"

"I assumed it!" the youth cried. All his respect was now turned into animal defense. "Don't you suppose anyone could see what you're driving at? You're trying to put the blame on me! And you can't do it! You can't do it!"

Meade was silent now for a few moments, but his eyes did not leave Crane. They bored into him more fiercely than any spoken accusation. Crane was pallid and his fists were clenched and white at his sides. He stood there, swaying a little; eyes, wide and frightened, fixed on President Meade. The president suddenly stabbed a forefinger at him and shot out:

"Crane, you'll tell what you know! If you're innocent of any complicity in this murder—and it *is* murder—then you'll tell what you're hiding. And if you won't tell, it won't take the police long to assume that what you are hiding is the fact that you killed Professor Yerkes yourself! Come now—I want the truth!"

The president had half risen from his chair and he was flushed and his every word was a threat to Crane. The youth swayed a little, stiffened with a perceptible effort, and he cried out in a voice almost hysterical:

"I've nothing to tell! I don't know anything! You can do what you please! I've nothing to tell!"

He reached suddenly for the edge of the desk, as if to steady himself, and the next moment collapsed in a faint. Dr. Royal caught him quickly as he fell.

Ingram stepped hastily to the window and threw it up, for the air was stale and warm. The doctor seated Crane in a chair and opened his collar. Ingram hastened away for a tumbler of water. The doctor opened a vial of aromatic spirits of ammonia and held it to Crane's nostrils.

The president went out into the corridor and strode up and down nervously. He was an educator, not a criminologist, and he was at the end of his rope. Crane might well have fainted simply from excitement rather than from any fear of being found out. The president had muddled the task. He knew it and felt helpless.

The doctor had brought Crane to his senses when Meade went into the office again. Ingram stood by, watching as the youth opened his eyes.

Crane got up from the chair with an effort.

"I want to go home," he said. "I want to go to my room. I want to get out of here."

"Better sit down and rest a while," the doctor advised.

"I want to get out of here," Crane insisted, his lip trembling.

"You aren't in condition to go home yet," the doctor insisted. "Rest a while."

"I'm all right," Crane protested weakly. "I'm all right. I just want some air. I don't need any rest. I can walk home. I can walk home alone. Let me go."

He thrust away the doctor's supporting hand and started out the door. He went slowly across the corridor, looking neither to the right nor to the left. He went out into the lane and the door closed behind him.

Meade said to the doctor: "Well, what do you think?"

Dr. Royal shook his head. "I don't know what to think. That lad is in bad physical condition. Looks undernourished. Any one in that condition might have fainted as he did—innocent or guilty."

Meade nodded, stood looking gloomily at the floor. "And I suppose it's possible," he declared, "that he left his notebook in the study room, say, yesterday; or even that someone else put it there."

"It's possible."

"And it is also possible," Meade said to Ingram, "that there was someone else—not Crane—in that study room when you arrived—someone who went out not by the front door but by the basement exit and through the grass and bushes there."

"That may be," Ingram replied.

"The rear door would be the better way out for one who was trying to leave without being seen."

"I suppose so."

"In other words, it is quite possible that Crane was telling the truth—that he wasn't here at all, but that when you saw him, he was merely coming past the building."

"Certainly it's possible."

The president resumed his pacing up and down, hands clasped behind his back.

"In the face of this serious business," he said, "I think it is imperative that we consider every possibility. It is quite possible that that young man was telling the truth and the entire truth, but—" he halted suddenly and wheeled to face Professor Ingram and Dr. Royal—"gentlemen, I don't believe it. I believe that he was lying. Whether he is the murderer or not, we can't say. But I believe that he was lying and that it was fear of being found out that worked him up so and caused him to faint."

Neither Ingram nor Royal made reply. The doctor said, after an interval during which Ingram closed the window and turned his back to it: "I think, Dr. Meade, that you ought to notify the police now. They won't relish this delay."

"Who cares what they relish!" Meade snapped. Then, as if thinking better of it, he sat down before the telephone. "I believe you're right," he admitted at length. He drew a deep breath of resignation and defeat and picked up the receiver. "Get me police headquarters, at once. This is President Meade speaking."

# 5
## WEDNESDAY 4:40 P.M.


Besides notifying police headquarters, President Meade telephoned directly to the district attorney's office. The district attorney, Kent Bloomingdale, had been a personal friend of Yerkes's. They had become acquainted and friendly during those cases which Yerkes had solved.

President Meade talked with Bloomingdale personally. Shortly Bloomingdale was on his way to the university in a police car, along with the medical examiner, Dr. Thayer, Captain Packer of the homicide squad, and two patrolmen in plain clothes.

In another car, following, came Casey, police photographer, Munyon, fingerprint expert, two patrolmen in uniform, and a plainclothes man driving.

In the first car, the medical examiner was quizzing the district attorney.

"I don't know a thing," Bloomingdale told him. "All I got is that somebody shot Yerkes—in his office, and that they haven't the faintest idea who did it."

Bloomingdale was tall and exceedingly thin. He had a beaklike nose, a large, thin-lipped mouth, and small black eyes that were sharp and nervous as the eyes of a mouse. Bloomingdale had liked Yerkes. He had admired the manner in which the man had, time and again, gone forward in what seemed to be blind alleys and found a way through to the truth. He was exceedingly regretful that such a man had met his end, and he was voicing that regret to the doctor and voicing also the same thought that Ingram had put forth: that Yerkes had likely been murdered by some one into whose past he, Yerkes, had been delving. Bloomingdale, however, did not have any idea, as Ingram did, concerning any specific case Yerkes might have been handling.

"There are two classes of people, doctor," Bloomingdale said to Thayer, "who might have wanted to take Yerkes's life. One group would be those whose crimes he had already found out and brought to—to justice; another would be those who feared he would find them out. . . . Those who wanted revenge or those who wanted to forestall him."

"Which ones do you consider most dangerous to you?" the doctor inquired. "The ones you have put away or the ones you are seeking out?"

"I'd sooner take my chance," Bloomingdale said, "with the ones I've put away. What they hold is a grudge, and grudges wear off. But these others—say, a murderer who is afraid I'll get him—there's the man I'd put nothing past."

"Then the first thing to find out, perhaps," the doctor summed up, "is whether Yerkes was working on a case the outcome of which meant trouble, serious trouble, for someone. Perhaps if you can find the case and that someone, you'll have Yerkes's murderer."

Bloomingdale nodded. He said thoughtfully: "Yerkes was a remarkable fellow. I don't think he knew the meaning of fear. The day we pulled in that Hooper kleptomaniac youngster, the boy drew a gun and said he'd shoot the first one that came near him. Yerkes walked right up to him, talking to him as you'd talk to an excited animal to calm it down, and he took the gun right out of the boy's hand, as nice as pie. I stood there with a sweat on me, I tell you; but not Yerkes. He had a lot of nerve. He should never have spent his life as a college professor. He liked the excitement of criminal investigation too much."

On the other side of the doctor, sitting motionless, cigar butt clamped between his teeth, hands folded in his lap, blue eyes staring straight ahead past the driver's shoulder to the road, was Captain Packer. Since these two had begun to chat, he had listened in complete silence. Now Bloomingdale leaned forward and said to him:

"Well, what have you got to say, Packer? You knew Yerkes."

Packer took the cigar from his mouth, nodding gravely.

"I knew him well," he said. "He was a fine man. He showed me a thing or two. But I don't know yet what to think."

They were traveling along Farragut Avenue at a good rate, when, just east of Paisley Road, Bloomingdale said to the driver: "Take the next right. Paisley Road." The car made the turn. "It's that pathway on the right. That yellow building. Pull up there." The car swung up to the curb beside Chatham Lane and stopped.

Bloomingdale, the medical examiner and the captain got out. Bloomingdale said to one plainclothes man: "You'd better come along. You"—to the driver—"wait for the other car and tell them to hop right in." He turned away and went down the lane. The others followed.

As they neared the door to Chatham House, it opened and there on the threshold stood President Meade, grave faced.

"Afternoon, Dr. Meade," Bloomingdale greeted. "Where is he—Yerkes? Upstairs in his office, you said?"

President Meade stepped aside. "Yes, upstairs in his office." Then, in a confidential tone, he said: "Oh, Mr. Bloomingdale," and drew the district attorney aside. "I wonder if we can manage to go through with this investigation with a minimum of publicity. You understand. Publicity of this sort is not good for a university."

"I understand," Bloomingdale said. "I'll do all I can for you. There's no muzzling the reporters, though. Treat them fairly and they'll treat you fairly. That's all you can expect. And I'll go as easy as I can."

"Thank you," said President Meade a little sadly.

Bloomingdale turned away. He said to the patrolman in plain clothes: "Caffrey, no one goes in or out of this door without my permission or Captain Packer's. No exceptions."

"Yes, sir," said Caffrey.

"And, by the way," Bloomingdale asked Meade, "is there another exit from this place?"

The president nodded. "In the basement. A rear door. The stairway to the basement is there."

Bloomingdale said to Caffrey: "Call in Murphy. Tell him to find that exit downstairs and stay there. Nobody in, nobody out."

"Yes, sir," said Caffrey.

# 6
## WEDNESDAY 5:05 P.M.


Ingram sat alone in his office. President Meade was out in the corridor conferring with the police. Through the closed door Ingram could hear the voice of the district attorney giving instructions to let no one in and no one out.

He sat looking fixedly out the window, pondering, judging himself. At length he got up and went out into the corridor. The president was pacing back and forth again, nervously. Caffrey, the plainclothes man was standing inside the front entrance, watching the president, who was ignoring him completely.

Ingram started for the stairway. The president looked up.

"They'll probably want to talk with me," Ingram said. The president nodded. Ingram went upstairs, the steps creaking under his tread. Just as he reached the landing, Captain Packer came out of Yerkes's office.

He said: "We want to talk with the man who found him. Professor Ingram, the doctor says."

"My name is Ingram."

Bloomingdale came to the door of the office.

"Mind stepping in here for a few minutes, professor?" he asked. "Just a few questions."

Ingram went in. The medical examiner was bending over the body. Dr. Royal stood at one side.

"I'm the district attorney," said Bloomingdale. "Suppose you tell us about it, professor."

Ingram did so. He gave his story as he had given it to President Meade, no more, no less, except that he told about looking for Schultz the janitor. Bloomingdale asked for the note Yerkes had left under Ingram's door and Ingram passed it over to him. "President Meade has Crane's notebook," he said.

Bloomingdale said: "I wish you'd send for this Luciano and Crane. Can we get them right away?"

"I'll ask the dean's office to have them located. Then do you want me to stay around?"

"For a while, please."

"Very well." Ingram went downstairs and telephoned the dean's office.

In the meantime the second police car arrived and the photographer and fingerprint man went upstairs. Ingram followed and stood outside the door while the photographer took pictures from many angles and the fingerprint man went over the room with a powerful lens and took a number of photographs of fingerprints on the desk, on the telephone, on the door and on several objects on the desk.

"Of course," the captain grumbled to Ingram, "you've probably spoiled any fingerprints that may have been on the telephone or on the doorknob—and elsewhere."

"I'm sorry," Ingram said.

The medical examiner had been going through Yerkes's pockets. He turned out, among other articles, a roll of bills totaling thirty-two dollars. "There's your motive of robbery gone," he said. "Here's some jewelry too: ring, watch and charm. Well, my story's this. He was shot as he sat in this chair—right through the heart. The bullet is imbedded in the back of the chair. You didn't find the gun, did you? It was a forty-five, I should judge. He probably never knew what hit him. He just fell forward on the desk. There are no powder marks on his clothes. The killer probably stood about there, across the desk from him, probably six feet or more away."

"How long ago did death occur?" Packer asked.

"About a couple of hours—near as I can say," Dr. Thayer ventured.

The captain turned to Ingram. "And what time did you find him?" he asked.

"Three-twenty."

The captain grumbled. "You wasted some valuable time before notifying us."

President Meade had come up the stairs. "I'll assume responsibility for that," he put in. "I delayed calling you, in the hope that we could get the truth ourselves and—ah—just turn the culprit over to you."

Packer scowled. "You think the police will be all year doing it, do you?"

The president said nothing.

"I'd like a place to speak with these two men, Crane and Luciano, when they come," Bloomingdale said. "Is there an empty office or—"

"Use mine—downstairs," Ingram offered.

"Thanks. Let's go down there now and give these men a chance to finish up their work."

Captain Packer led the way downstairs, and while the others went into Ingram's office, Packer walked to the head of the basement stairway.

"Murphy," he called, "are you down there?"

"Yes, sir," said Murphy. "Down here at the back door."

Captain Packer descended. "Where's that janitor's place?" he asked.

Murphy pointed to the end of the corridor. "Must be there. The rest of this place is just bins."

Packer opened the door that looked out into the thicket behind Chatham House. He followed the path with his eyes, slowly, till it turned and went out of sight. Then he closed the door and walked down towards the janitor's quarters.

He had no better luck than Ingram. The knob rattled and that was all. But Packer did more than Ingram had done. He leaned to the door and placed an ear against it. He listened for nearly a minute, then turned away, frowning. He returned to the rear door of the building and opened it once more.

Now he stepped out on to the path and walked slowly along it, studying the ground as he went. Now and then he stopped and looked from left to right over the bushes and grass. When he reached the group of trees in the center of the thicket, he paused, glanced up at the tree branches overhead; rubbed his jaw thoughtfully, then went on down the narrow path.

Twice from here to the road he stopped, turned about and stood looking at the rear wall of Chatham House. Then, after a brief glance up and down Paisley Road, he entered the path again and returned to the building, went upstairs and down the corridor to Ingram's office.

"Find anything?" Bloomingdale asked him.

The captain shook his head. "There's a path down there from the rear door to the road. Easy getaway—covered by that tall grass, if one wanted to keep from being seen. Anyone could have got away, professor," he said to Ingram, "even with you right here looking out the window—provided they just ducked low in the grass and bushes out there."

"Yes," Ingram agreed. "I suppose so."

Bloomingdale glanced at his watch. Just then Caffrey let Luciano in at the front door.

"In there," Caffrey said, jerking a thumb towards Ingram's office.

Luciano came across the corridor with silent step and Packer stood in Ingram's doorway as he approached. President Meade looked past Packer. "Here's Luciano," he announced.

"Come in," said Packer, and stood aside. Bloomingdale was seated at Ingram's desk. He looked up at the student and a little frown came into his eyes.

"Luciano?"

"Yes, sir."

"Luciano, I'm the district attorney. . . . Tell me, Luciano, where have I seen you before?"

Luciano shook his head slowly. "I'm sure I don't know."

Bloomingdale's sharp eyes searched Luciano's face. "I don't either. You remind me of someone, though. That's it. Who would it be?"

"I'm sorry—I don't know," Luciano replied.

Bloomingdale fingered a pencil. "You were in this building earlier this afternoon, weren't you?" he asked.

"Twice before this," Luciano stated. "Once to deposit a theme, the second time at President Meade's order."

"The first visit was at what time?"

"A little after three, I believe."

"Did you meet anyone coming in or going out of the building? Did you see anyone else here?"

"No one. But as I told Dr. Meade, I did hear voices in here. From upstairs."

"Whose voices?"

"I'm quite sure one was Professor Yerkes's. I believe there were two others, but I don't know whose they were."

"That was at what time? Can you say exactly?"

"Not exactly. Probably five minutes after three."

"Tell us what you did in the building."

"I put a theme in Professor Bailey's box. I glanced over it for a minute or so, then dropped it in the box."

"Then did you leave immediately?"

"Yes, sir."

"Didn't go into any of the rooms here?"

"No, sir."

Bloomingdale held Luciano's eye. "Do you know," he asked in a matter of fact voice, "that a murder has been committed here?"

Luciano's eyes widened. He shook his head. "I didn't know that. I knew, from what Dr. Meade said, that something had happened, but I didn't know it was murder. Who—who was killed?"

Bloomingdale told him: "Professor Yerkes."

Luciano echoed: "Professor Yerkes!" And his mouth fell open in amazement.

"Luciano," Bloomingdale pursued, "how well did you know Professor Yerkes?"

Luciano stared. "Why, I knew him scarcely at all."

"When you say scarcely at all, just what do you mean?"

"Why, I knew him by sight—everybody did, I suppose, here at the University; but I had never taken a course with him."

"Yet you're quite sure it was his voice you heard from upstairs?"

"Well, yes, sir. You see, he had a peculiarly characteristic voice—thin and sharp, with a nasal or metallic quality. I thought I knew his voice, sir. I've heard him speak to others many times."

Bloomingdale laid down his pencil. "Got anything else to offer?" he asked. "Anything you think we ought to know?"

"No, sir. Except that I met Professor Ingram in East Park. He was coming this way. There isn't anything else I can think of."

"All right," Bloomingdale dismissed him. "That'll do. I may call on you again. That's all."

Luciano said: "Yes, sir," and went out of the office, a faintly bewildered look on his face.

When Luciano had left the building, Captain Packer went out into the corridor.

"Where," he asked Ingram, "is the theme box he spoke about? Professor Bailey's theme box." Ingram led the way to a row of theme boxes on the south wall of the corridor, to the left of the vestibule as they faced it. "Professor Bailey's is the third one, I believe."

Packer tried the lid of the box. "Locked," he said. "Who has the key? Professor Bailey?"

Ingram nodded.

"Where can we get hold of Bailey?"

"Probably at his home," Ingram replied. "I'm going that way if you people can spare me. Shall I stop in and tell him you'd like to have the key?"

"You might do that," the captain agreed, "if it's all right with Mr. Bloomingdale." He went back to the office. "Do you need Professor Ingram any more?" he inquired.

"I guess not," Bloomingdale decided. "But hold yourself available, professor, please."

"Certainly."

The telephone on the desk rang. Bloomingdale answered it. When he hung up he said: "It was the dean's office. They've had a messenger out trying to locate Crane. They can't find him." He looked at Meade. "What does that mean, Dr. Meade? Ordinarily would your dean's office be able to locate him?'"

Meade shook his head. "Not at all times. If he went for a walk, or to someone else's room without leaving word with any one, they might not be able to get him at once."

"Doesn't he have a roommate who might know where he is?"

"Probably."

"Well, I want the roommate located then, please."

"Very well. Let me have the phone and I'll see what can be done."

Dr. Meade was snapping curtly into the telephone as Ingram took his leave. Upstairs he could hear the voices of the finger-print man and the photographer. Yerkes's body was still there. Ingram shuddered a little as he went across the vestibule and out into Chatham Lane.

# 7
## WEDNESDAY 6:10 P.M.

Ingram went out to Paisley Road, walked north till he came to Aldrich Road, which made a left turn from Paisley and followed North Park the full length of the northern end of the campus. Leading off Aldrich Road was Price Street, and on this street Professor Bailey lived.

The house was a large and old one, set back from the street about twenty yards. Professor Ingram went in at the gate and would have gone directly up the path to the door but that a voice halted him. It was Mary Bailey.

"Hello, Ben," she called. Ingram turned. She was standing under a tree down at the further end of the yard. She was wearing a blue gingham dress and carried a garden spade.

"Hello, Mary." Mary was tall, brown-haired, sweet of face. She approached, smiling.

"How are you, you old bear?" she said. "I'm off your social list, I suppose. I haven't seen you in nearly a week."

He shook his head gravely. "I've been very busy. I've wanted to come and see you several times, but I haven't been able to get away."

"The gallant professor!" she laughed. "You haven't wanted to see me nor any other woman. How can you be such a hermit?"

He smiled. It was a sober smile. "If you'd make up your mind and marry me," he said, "then perhaps I wouldn't be a hermit. That makes nine times I've asked now."

She laughed softly.

"Is it nine?" she asked.

"What's my lucky number?" he wanted to know.

"Who can tell?" She grinned broadly.

"Perhaps—someday?" he insisted, his smile gone, his manner intensely serious.

"Perhaps," she repeated. "Someday."

He wanted to take care of her. There was trouble ahead. He said earnestly: "There isn't anyone else, is there?"

"There certainly isn't," she replied. "When I get ready to marry—though heaven knows when that will be—it's going to be you, if I have to club and bind you to get you."

He smiled with much relief. "I wish I knew you meant that."

"I do," she told him. "Don't you see, a girl wants freedom for a certain length of time—just as much as a man. You're thirty-five. You're still free."

"That's your fault," he said. "I've been waiting for you. Let me get you a ring, Mary. Then you'll be free for as long as you please, but I'll know better how matters stand with us."

"No girl wearing an engagement ring is free," she said. "I've still got a lot of running around to do with exciting men. Exciting men that no one would ever think of marrying. You aren't exciting at all, you know, Ben. You don't care about dancing, you never drive at eighty miles an hour, you never—"

He was suddenly stern. "If I ever catch you driving at eighty miles an hour," he warned, "I'll—"

"You'll never catch me," she laughed. "You see, you'd have to drive faster to do it."

"Someday I'll think of a way to be exciting," he said.

She laid a hand on his arm. "Don't," she urged. "I'd rather have you just as you are. That sounds as if I want everything, doesn't it? Well, I do, I guess."

"I think you do," he smiled. "And I hope you get exactly what you deserve."

"In the long run," she told him, "I hope I can deserve you."

"I'm blushing," he said. "And I'm through joking with you. I want to see your father."

She stared at him. "Funny, the way you said that. You got dark as a rain cloud all of a sudden."

"Did I? Tell me, is your father in?"

"Yes. I'll see if I can find him for you. Come in." They went in together. She went upstairs and returned to tell him that her father would see him in the study. "Father looks tired," she remarked. "And worried. I wonder what it can be."

Upstairs Ingram found Professor Bailey standing before the window in his study. Bailey was a short, gray man with kindly blue eyes; eyes that were troubled now as he turned to greet Ingram.

"Hello, Ben, Sit down. Want to see me about something?"

Ingram stood inside the door. "Mind if I close this?"

"Not at all," Bailey replied. Something in Ingram's manner seemed to put him on his guard. The gloom of late afternoon was beginning to come. Bailey walked forward to his desk and turned on a light there. Ingram noticed that his hand trembled as he did so. Bailey moved away again towards the shadow of a bookcase. He made a pretense of straightening a row of books, his back to Ingram.

At length he turned. "Ben, what is it? This isn't merely social. I can tell by your manner. Come, out with it."

Ingram asked: "Have you heard what's happened?"

"No. What is it?"

"Something pretty terrible." His eyes searched Bailey's face. "Yerkes has been murdered."

"Murdered!" Bailey started forward a pace, then halted. "By whom?"

"The police are there," Ingram said. "They don't know who did it."

"Where did it happen—when—and how?"

"Chatham House, this afternoon. I found him in his office, shot through the heart."

"Oh! And they haven't any idea who did it?"

"None."

"Good heavens—what could anyone have killed him for?"

"I don't know."

"Poor old Yerkes." Bailey fumbled for a cigar in his pocket, bit off the end and struck a match to light it. His nervous fingers dropped the match. He stepped hastily on it as it fell to the hardwood floor at the edge of the rug. "You found him? Tell me about it."

"I walked over to Chatham House at about three," Ingram explained. "I was in my office for a short time, then went upstairs to see Yerkes. I found him. He was dead."

Bailey shook his head dumbly.

"Uncle Hardy," Ingram asked, "did you have any conferences there this afternoon?"

"You know I never have Wednesday afternoon conferences. No, I didn't go to Chatham this afternoon. Poor old Yerkes. There was a brilliant man, Ben. Murdered! That's terrible!"

"Have you been to your theme box this afternoon?" Ben pursued.

"I told you I hadn't been there this afternoon." This a little impatiently. "Why do you ask?"

Ingram was silent for several seconds. He hated this, but it had to be done.

"The police," he said at length, "want the key to your theme box."

"And why," Bailey demanded, "should they want that?"

"To corroborate the story of one of the students who says he deposited a theme in your box around three o'clock. It probably won't signify anything, but the police captain there wants to check up on all details. He asked for the key. I told him I'd tell you he wanted it."

"Who is the student?"

"Luciano—Guido Luciano."

Bailey said, after a pause: "You mean that if no theme is found in the box—no theme of Luciano's—his story will be discredited?"

"I believe so."

"What story did he tell?"

"He says he dropped into Chatham House to put his theme in the box and then left the building. Says he knows nothing of the murder. Will you send over the key?"

Bailey frowned thoughtfully for a moment or two.

"I'm sorry about this, Ben," he began. "It's unfortunate it had to be now—but you see, I haven't had that key since yesterday. I've lost it—or mislaid it. Tell you what—I'll phone and tell them to force the box if they want to do that."

His eye did not meet Ingram's. And Ingram did not believe this story about the key. Bailey had not lost it. He was lying, a lie consistent with his backdoor retreat from Chatham House. If the box was forced now and no theme found, Luciano's story would be discredited. The police would scarcely be shrewd enough to see that the circumstance might be interpreted the other way, to involve Bailey.

Ingram said: "Uncle Hardy, I don't like to bring this up, but—" He hesitated, paused.

Bailey said: "Yes? What is it?"

Ingram walked to the window, uneasy, unhappy. He saw Mary down there, standing by the fence.

Bailey repeated: "Yes? What is it you were going to say?"

"I was considering," Ingram replied, without turning, "whether to say it or not."

Professor Bailey came quickly to his side.

"What is it?" he demanded. "If it's something I must know—"

"It's something we both know already. You and I and another."

"Who's the other—and what is it?"

"The other," Ingram informed him, "is Professor Davis."

There was a brief silence. Then Bailey said: "And what is it we all know?"

"Something," Ingram declared reluctantly, "that we would all like to forget. You and Professor Davis were at Chatham House together this afternoon. I saw you there. I saw you through my window. You were leaving through the thicket at the rear." He had turned now to face Bailey.

Bailey's mouth twitched and hardened. He said quickly: "That's not true."

Ingram moved away from him, towards the desk. He laid a hand on the telephone there. "May I phone Professor Davis?" he asked. "He ought to come here while we talk this over."

Bailey was looking out the window. "There's no need," he stated quietly. "He's coming in at the gate this very moment."

They stood thus, listening, and heard the sound of Mary's voice in the hallway below and the voice of Professor Davis. Then, a knock on the door.

"Come in," said Bailey from the window.

The door opened and Professor Davis came in. For a moment or two his tall, wiry-looking figure was framed in the doorway. His deep-set eyes went from Ingram to Bailey. He said: "Good evening, Ben." Then his eyes met Bailey's. He closed the door.

"Good evening, Uncle Tad," Ben murmured. "You're just in time. I was going to phone you."

"Yes? What for?" His eyes sought Bailey's again.

"You know, don't you," Ingram went on, "that Philip Yerkes was murdered this afternoon?"

Davis stood quite still. "No!" he exclaimed softly in a moment. "Is that really true?"

"It's really true. He was murdered at Chatham House."

"By whom?"

Ingram ignored the question. "Uncle Tad, I saw you and Uncle Hardy going away from Chatham House shortly, I believe, after Yerkes was killed. I saw you in the thicket behind the building. You don't deny that, do you?"

Davis came forward swiftly. "Deny it!" he cried. "Certainly I deny it! You may have seen us there in the thicket. We were there. We went for a walk. We walked into the thicket, then walked back. We didn't go as far as the building. Isn't that so, Hardy?"

Bailey said in an unconvincing tone: "Why—yes—that's right. We walked into the thicket, then went back." His face was white in the shadows of the room. "Ben, you don't think—?"

He looked at Ingram, the rest of the question unspoken.

"I don't know what to think," Ingram returned. "I'm trying hard to think of you—both of you—and of Mary and Mrs. Davis. That's why I'm bewildered. I really am bewildered. For I don't know what to believe. If there's any explanation—"

Davis said: "There's no explanation. We've told you all there is to tell."

"You really want me to believe, then, that you went into that thicket merely for a walk? That's pretty hard to believe, Uncle Tad. The walking is very poor there."

Thaddeus Davis said hotly: "Believe what you like Why should you question us like this? Have you set yourself up with the police and—?"

Bailey raised a hand. "Tad, just a moment. Ben, in a more or less indirect way, you are accusing us of Yerkes's murder. That's what's in your mind, isn't it?"

Ingram threw out a hand in a gesture of helplessness. "No!" he cried. "Heaven knows I don't want to see any blame on you, either of you. But I do want you to explain your hurried departure from the building there by the back way. If you've done nothing, you ought to give me the truth. You see, by my testimony either Luciano or Crane may be implicated, possibly accused and arrested, probably sent to the electric chair. And all the while I have kept silent about two who acted far more suspiciously than either Crane or Luciano. This thing is on my head. I want some justification for what I have done. If you have an explanation, I want it."

"And if you don't get one," Davis wanted to know, "what'll you do?"

"What can I do? What course do you leave me?"

Bailey came forward now. His face had turned ashen. The hand that he placed upon Ingram's arm shook violently. "Ben," he pleaded, "please think well before you do anything."

"What," Davis insisted, "do you intend to do?"

"What do you intend to tell me?" Ingram countered.

"There's nothing to tell," Davis returned.

Ingram turned away. In agitation he strode to the far end of the room near the windows, then came back. He halted before these two, whose eyes were fixed upon him.

"Tell me," he demanded, "did you—did either of you kill Philip Yerkes?"

Bailey turned away at the question. He looked sick. He went to the chair behind his desk and sat down slowly, almost feebly, as an invalid would seat himself. Davis remained standing, glaring at Ingram.

"No!" Davis said. "Whether you believe it or not—no!"

There was a silence now. The clock on the desk ticked away the seconds. Then Bailey said in a trembling voice: "Go away, Ben. Please go away."

"But what am I to do?" Ingram asked. "A child could tell that you are hiding the truth."

"You don't believe me," Davis asked, "when I say that we had nothing to do with the murder?"

Ingram made no reply, but his silence told what he thought. "You don't make it easy for me to believe," he said at length.

"What are you going to do?" Bailey asked, his voice listless.

Ingram moved slowly towards the door. When he reached it, he placed a hand upon the knob, then faced them once more.

"Nothing," he said soberly. "I'm going to do nothing. Nothing at all."

He went out and closed the door behind him. The stairway was unlighted and somber, and the hall below. He went out of the house and up the path to the street. Mary was not there, and he was glad of that, for he could not have raised his spirits to meet hers.

# 8
## WEDNESDAY 6:45 P.M.

Ingram went back to Chatham House. As he came down Paisley Road, he saw a crowd of students and a number of cars in the road beside the house. Some of the cars bore stickers marked "Press." He turned into the lane. There were lights in the lower and upper corridors, in Yerkes's office.

As he made his way through the groups in front of the door, someone touched his arm and said: "Hello, professor. My name's Hubbard. I'm from the *Record*. Will you give me a statement? I understand you found the body."

Other reporters gathered about. Ingram shook his head.

"I'm afraid," he said, "I'm not authorized to say anything. You'll have to see President Meade or the district attorney."

"The D. A." said another reporter, "seems to have given out orders to play deaf and dumb. He blames it on Meade too. Aren't the citizens entitled to the news any more? This is pretty irregular."

"Sorry." Ingram moved to the door, the newspaper men following him. He tried the door and suddenly Caffrey pulled it open and glared at him.

"I told you guys—" He halted. "Oh, you, professor. They want you in here?"

"I've something to tell Captain Packer. Something he wanted to know."

Caffrey stepped aside. "Okay, come in, professor." Then, to the reporters who crowded close behind: "Nix! Have a heart, you guys! Orders is orders. Wouldn't I let you in if I could?"

"You wouldn't let your uncle in to see your aunt," said one of the reporters in the back of the group.

"Just a wise guy!" Caffrey retorted. "Just an old-fashioned wise guy!"

By this time the foremost reporter was standing on the threshold trying to look past Caffrey across the vestibule. Caffrey placed a big palm gently on his chest and shoved him out.

"Don't push me!" cried the reporter. "That's a battery and you know it."

"Sue me," Caffrey replied and closed the door. The latch clicked.

There was a light going in Ingram's office and the door was open. Captain Packer came out to see what the commotion was.

"Hello, professor," he said. "You want to see me?"

"Yes. Professor Bailey says, captain, that he misplaced the key to his theme box some time yesterday, but he says you may force the lid of the box if you please."

"Lost his key, eh?" The captain went to the row of theme boxes. "Is this the one—the one marked English 2?"

"That's it." Ingram stood beside the captain as the latter tried to peer into the slot in the top of the box. Packer looked up and said:

"Got a paper knife or something I can force it with?"

"In my office. I'll get it for you." Ingram went across the corridor to his office. President Meade, sitting at the desk, soberly chewing a cold cigar, nodded to him. Ingram opened a drawer and took out a bronze paper knife. He returned to Captain Packer and gave it to him. The lock was a flimsy one and gave way easily. The lid sprang up as the lock broke. Packer thrust his hand in, felt around, then looked up at Ingram.

"There's nothing in it," he said. "Not a thing." He went away abruptly then, along the corridor and upstairs. Ingram heard him talking with Bloomingdale. They came downstairs together.

"Get Luciano again," Bloomingdale said. "And this time we'll find out what's what. So he lied about the theme, eh? Caffrey, go to this address and get Guido Luciano. And lock that front door on your way out and get back as soon as you can. And you, captain, will you please phone to headquarters for some more men? We're shorthanded here. We haven't got Crane yet, either. Fine efficiency. Nor his roommate. Caffrey, look up Leonard Crane's address in the directory in Professor Ingram's office and bring him over too. And hustle, will you?"

There was a knock at the outer door and Caffrey hastened to open it. A thin, bony youth stood there, sloppily dressed, hands thrust deep in the pockets of a baggy topcoat. He wore a soiled felt hat with its brim pressed up flat against the crown in front. His mouth opened in awe as Caffrey demanded: "What do you want?"

"I—I don't want anything," the youth said. "I'm Leonard Crane's roommate. Messenger from the dean's office said I was wanted over here."

Caffrey stepped aside. The reporters pressed forward. The student entered. Caffrey stepped into the breach and a groan went up.

"Aw, break down, Caffrey!" . . . "Give in, will ya?"

"Nerts!" said Caffrey and closed the door.

Bloomingdale said to Caffrey: "Better wait around a few minutes." To Crane's roommate he said: "This way," and led the way into Ingram's office. He seated himself. The student was nervous.

"What's your name?" Bloomingdale asked.

"Beasley. Robert C. Beasley. What's the matter, anyway? Has something happened to Leonard?"

"You mean Crane?" Beasley nodded. "What makes you think something's happened to him?"

"Oh, I don't know," Beasley replied. "But I haven't seen him all afternoon. He usually comes back to the room at six—and it's after that now."

"And he didn't come back tonight?"

"No, sir. I came in myself a little before six. He wasn't there. I found a message from the dean's office on the door, and just then a messenger came in again. He said you wanted Leonard too, so I waited around a while, and when he didn't come, I left a note for him and came over myself. I don't know what's the matter. He usually comes in at six almost on the dot and we go to dinner together."

Ingram glanced at his wrist watch. It was five minutes before seven.

Bloomingdale said: "I want you to do something for us, Beasley. I want you to locate Crane as promptly as you can, and when you find him, tell him he's wanted here without delay. And another thing. I don't want you to talk to anybody about this. Just try to locate Crane and bring him here. Come back yourself with him. Understand?"

"Yes, sir. What's happened here, sir? Somebody killed?"

"We'll explain all about it later."

"Yes, sir." Beasley turned to go.

"Beasley." It was President Meade. He was standing in the doorway of Ingram's office. "Beasley, you'll cooperate to the letter with the district attorney. To the letter, mind."

"Yes, Dr. Meade," Beasley said, even more awed. "Yes, sir, I understand. I'm to get Leonard Crane and bring him back here and not talk to anyone about anything—about any of this."

"That's it," said Meade.

Beasley went hastily across the corridor. Caffrey opened the outer door and Beasley slipped out. Caffrey asked Bloomingdale, who had come into the corridor: "Shall I go and find Luciano now?"

"Go ahead," Bloomingdale said.

Caffrey went out. Bloomingdale asked Ingram: "Professor, can you give me any information about this Luciano? What kind of person is he? Have you got any line on him at all?"

Ingram replied: "I don't know much about him. He took a course with me last year and came to conference with me several times during that course, but I know nothing about his personal affairs."

"What about Crane? Know anything about him?"

"Nothing."

Meade asked: "You think, Mr. Bloomingdale, that the reason Crane hasn't showed up is that he's implicated—that he's the murderer, and has fled?"

"Possibly. If he's run away, I'll be annoyed but not surprised." Bloomingdale fell into thought for half a minute, then said to

Ingram: "Professor, will you please come upstairs to Yerkes's office for a few minutes. There's something I want to go over with you."

"Certainly." Ingram followed him upstairs and down to Yerkes's office. The door there stood open. Yerkes's body had been removed.

Bloomingdale stood aside for Ingram to pass in, then followed, closed the door and seated himself in a chair before the desk. It was not the chair in which Yerkes had died. That chair had been moved to a corner. Bloomingdale motioned Ingram to another chair on the other side of the desk. Ingram sat down.

Bloomingdale passed him a cigar and they lighted up in silence. At length Bloomingdale said: "Professor, I want your help."

"Yes?"

"Here's an odd thing," Bloomingdale continued. "On the way here from my office, I was saying to the medical examiner that if Yerkes had been murdered, it might have been done by someone who either had a grudge against him for, say, some crime he had pinned on him in the past, or else it was someone on whom he was about to pin a crime. And, oddly enough, the reason you offered as a plausible one for his addressing his note to you seems to coincide with that theory of mine. You mentioned that you were of the opinion Yerkes might have been investigating the theory of Professor Coombs's death. Now, if we go ahead on that theory, we come to a reasonable conclusion that Yerkes had ferreted out evidence against someone who thought Yerkes's possession of that evidence very dangerous. And that then that person put Yerkes out of the way to silence him. Now, the question is, have we any way of retracing the steps of Professor Yerkes to ascertain what that evidence was? Can you help? Have you any idea in just what direction he was working; whom he suspected; what he had done in his investigation?"

"No," Ingram replied. He tapped the ash off his cigar into a brass tray. "Yerkes took no one into his confidence—so far as I know."

Bloomingdale smoked and pondered for several seconds. "It strikes me," he said, "that if we could learn what enemies Coombs had, we might get a lead."

"Needle in a haystack," Ingram returned. "You see, Coombs was a cranky old man. He made many enemies with his tongue. He rarely meant the hard words he spoke, I am sure, but he spoke them nevertheless. He had more enemies, I believe, than friends. You'll find many that hated him, many that merely disliked him, and many who avoided him simply to avoid his insults. You'll find these among the faculty and in the student body. You'll find any number of them among the alumni. If you start looking among Coombs's enemies, you'll have a long search and a confusing one."

"I've found needles in haystacks before this, professor," Bloomingdale assured him. "Will you hold yourself ready to assist me if I should need you?"

"Yes," Ingram promised.

"Thanks." Bloomingdale glanced at his watch. There was a knock at the door. "Come in." It was Captain Packer.

"Excuse me," the captain said. "I've got something on my mind that's bothering me, and I wondered if you could explain it, professor."

"Yes?"

The captain closed the door. "This theme box business," he said. "Just how does it work? I mean, just when are students supposed to put themes into the box, and when are they collected, and who collects them?"

"That depends," Ingram informed him, "on the professor. In the various English courses, theme papers are required at certain intervals during the month and must be deposited in the theme box before a certain hour on the specified day. Either the professor or an assistant opens the box when the time is up and removes the papers of the entire class. Then there are make-up themes, or specially required themes. In such cases, and probably this was so in Luciano's case, the box might contain only one theme."

The captain's brow cleared. "That's what bothered me," he said. "I was thinking, if Luciano had to put a theme in the box, why, so would other students, and I was wondering where those other themes might be. I'd like to ask Professor Bailey if he had required a special theme from Luciano. Do you happen to know if he did?"

"No, I didn't ask."

The captain opened the door and stood listening. "There's someone just come in." He called down the stairway. "Is that you, Caffrey?"

"Yes, sir."

"Have you got Luciano there?"

"Yes, sir. He's here."

"Tell him to come up."

There was a light step on the stairs and then Luciano appeared at the door. He looked in questioningly. "Come in," Bloomingdale said.

Luciano walked in, hat in hand. His dark eyes were fixed on the district attorney. "We've a few more questions we want to ask you," Bloomingdale went on. "Particularly about that theme you said you came in to deposit at about three o'clock. You did say you came in to do that, didn't you?"

"Yes, of course I did."

"In Professor Bailey's box, eh?"

"Yes."

"And you're sure you put it in there?"

"Certainly."

"You didn't confuse the box? You didn't put it in another box by mistake?"

"No. I was quite careful to put it in the right box. It's the third box from the right as you face them. The third away from the vestibule. I was very particular to note that I was putting it in the right box because it's a theme on which I was granted extra time by Professor Bailey. He told me that if I didn't get it in today he wouldn't give me credit for it at all. I couldn't afford to be careless about the box I put it in. I need all my credits in that course."

"I see. By the way, what was the title of your theme?"

Luciano replied: "It was called The Movement to Abolish the Death Penalty."

Bloomingdale's eyebrows went up. "So! The Movement to Abolish the Death Penalty! Interesting! And did you defend that movement in the paper or did you stand against it?"

"I defended it."

"Hm! Why?"

"My chief reason was that it was better that a hundred villains should remain alive than that a single innocent man—convicted by circumstantial evidence—should be put to death."

"I see. What prompted the thought of such a paper, Luciano? Was it a required subject?"

"No. We were allowed to choose our own subjects. I happened to be discussing it with some of the fellows."

"I see. So you wrote your paper. Then you came over here at about three o'clock and dropped it in Professor Bailey's box. That's your story, as I understand it."

"Yes."

The district attorney leaned forward. He was all angles and loose at the joints. His eyes narrowed a little and he said:

"Luciano, we haven't been able to find that theme you speak about. We've opened the box, but your paper was not there."

Luciano declared firmly: "I put it there. Can I help it if it was taken away? Mr. District Attorney, are you trying to fasten this crime on me? If you are, I won't say another word until I've seen a reputable lawyer."

"Just a minute," Bloomingdale put in soothingly. "If you put the theme in the box and it isn't there now, there's evidently a good explanation for it. I'm simply asking you to help us. We've opened the box with Professor Bailey's permission and we find no theme. Can you suggest what may have happened to it?"

A strange light came into Luciano's eyes, as of an idea dawning.

"Yes," he stated quietly, "I think I can make a suggestion. Possibly Professor Bailey took that theme out of the box."

# 9
## WEDNESDAY 7:30 P.M.

The district attorney sat back in the chair and passed a hand over his chin. He said to Luciano: "So you think, do you, that Professor Bailey was here?"

Luciano shrugged. "I don't know of anyone else who might have access to the box. Professor Bailey collects his own themes. He doesn't have an assistant. If you didn't find my paper there, then Professor Bailey—or perhaps someone else, for all I know—removed it. At any rate, I put it there—whether you believe me or not."

"Oh, we believe you, Luciano," Bloomingdale said reassuringly. "We believe you, all right. Tell me a little more about this paper of yours. Was it typewritten?"

"Yes."

"Black ink?"

"No, blue. I have a blue ribbon on my machine."

"I see. On white typewriter paper?"

"Not ordinary typewriter paper. There are two holes punched in the margin so that it can be put in a looseleaf notebook."

"Do you happen to have a copy of it? You make a carbon copy, don't you?"

"Yes; it's in my room."

"Good. See that you don't lose it—in case we want it later. I think that's all for now, Luciano."

"Yes, sir." Luciano turned and went out.

Downstairs, President Meade came out of Ingram's office. "Luciano, just a moment."

"Yes, Dr. Meade?"

"Don't talk to the reporters," Meade ordered. "I will see personally that the press gets the necessary information at the proper time. You understand?"

"Certainly. Good night, Dr. Meade."

"Good night." President Meade went to the stairway and ascended wearily. He knocked at the broken door of Yerkes's office and Captain Packer opened.

"May I inquire," Meade asked, "whether you have made any progress?"

"Progress?" Bloomingdale echoed. "Oh, yes. We're getting somewhere. Slowly, perhaps; but we're moving. Things are beginning to take shape a little. I'll let you know when there's anything definite."

"Thank you. I'll go along now, I believe. You'll find me at home if you want me. Good evening."

"Good evening."

Meade went to the staircase. Then he returned to Yerkes's office. "And please," he begged unhappily, "be very careful—won't you, Mr. Bloomingdale?—about the information you give to the papers. We can't be too careful. The reputation of a great university is at stake."

"Rest assured," Bloomingdale said.

"Thank you. Good evening."

Packer closed the door now and stood with his back to it. Bloomingdale sat thinking for a few minutes, then looked up at Ingram. "Tell me about Professor Bailey, will you, Ingram?"

"What shall I tell you about him?"

"What kind of a man is he?"

"A very fine man."

"Professor of—?"

"English, of course. He is an authority on Shakespeare and Anglo-Saxon."

"You know him pretty well?"

"Very well."

"Do you happen to know how well acquainted he was with Yerkes?"

"Oh—he was always friendly with Yerkes. I don't believe they were very close, however."

"Ever hear of his having a run-in with Yerkes?"

"Never."

"How old a man is Bailey?"

"About sixty."

"Do you know anything about his relations with Professor Coombs?"

"Nothing very definite."

"Do you know what Coombs's opinion of him was?"

"No, I don't."

"You went over to his house earlier this evening and spoke to him about the key to the theme box, didn't you, professor?"

"I did."

"Did you mention the theme? Did you tell him why we wanted the key?"

"Yes. That was all right, wasn't it? I had to give him a reason for asking for it."

"Yes, it's all right. You say he said he had misplaced the key? That's what you told Captain Packer?"

"Yes. He said he hadn't had it since yesterday."

Bloomingdale leaned back in the chair, clasped lean hands behind his head and closed his eyes. He opened them at length, to fix them on Ingram.

"You see, don't you, professor, what this means? It means one of three things, any of which eliminates the others. First, say, Luciano lied about putting a theme in the box. Why he should lie about such a thing, I don't know. It's too easy a thing to check up on. I'm inclined to think that if he says he put a theme in that box, he most certainly did.

"Second possibility: Luciano did put the theme into the box and Professor Bailey took it out. By the way, did the professor say he had been here this afternoon, or hadn't? Did he make any statement to that effect?"

"I asked him that. He said he hadn't been here this afternoon."

"I see. Now, assume, in our second theory, that he did take out the theme. Why should he deny doing so? Well, it would mean that he had been here after Luciano left, or was here at the time. His voice may have been one of those that Luciano heard conversing with Yerkes. If Luciano heard Yerkes, that means Yerkes was murdered after Luciano left the building and before you reached it—a matter of how many minutes, professor?"

"One minute—approximately."

"We are assuming, for the time being," Bloomingdale said, "that Luciano's story is true and—"

Ingram interrupted: "But wouldn't I have heard a shot at that distance—even though the window was closed here?"

Bloomingdale shook his head. "Not necessarily. When you walk, are you in the habit"—he smiled a little—"of using your time in deeply concentrated thought?"

"I am," Ingram admitted. "I see."

"Well, the conclusion of my second temporary theory, professor, is that Professor Bailey was here and might have murdered Yerkes—or have been concerned in the murder."

Gravely Ingram inquired: "And your third theory?"

"Similar to the second. Credit Professor Bailey's statement that he has lost his key. Now—someone found it, or stole it—got it somehow—was here after Luciano left, opened the box and took out the theme—why, I don't know; probably to make Luciano's story appear a lie. That someone killed Yerkes and departed either by the front or rear door of the building."

Bloomingdale paused now. He turned in his chair to face Captain Packer. "What have you got to say about it, captain?"

Captain Packer grunted. "I want a look at Bailey," he stated, and Ingram's heart sank, "and a few words with him."

Bloomingdale got up. He thrust long fingers through his black hair. "And there's someone else we mustn't forget—that janitor—what's his name—Schultz? . . . Tell you what, captain. There's still this fellow Crane to wait for. I'll wait for him. Why don't you go over and see Bailey and have a talk with him. You'll take him over, professor? And, say—better send me in some food. I'm famished. Send me a club sandwich and a quart of coffee."

"All right," said Packer. "Coming, professor?"

They left Bloomingdale walking up and down in Yerkes's office. The light in the corridor below was pale, yellow. In the vestibule Caffrey blinked at them drowsily and opened the door.

There was a rush by the reporters. Behind them was a large group of students, hushed, listening, eager.

"What's the dope, captain?" a reporter asked. "Anything new?"

"Nothing new. Professor Yerkes is dead. He was murdered. With a gun. That's all."

"We knew that hours ago."

"So did we," the captain countered. "We don't know anything else yet."

"I'll take that on rye," said Hubbard of the *Record*.

A flashlight glared. "Thanks for the pitcher." Then in a softer voice, to some of the students: "Somebody gimme the name of the professor, will you?"

Two more lights. Two more pictures. The captain and Professor Ingram had reached the end of the lane. Another photographer backed away in front of them.

"Take some pictures of the building," the captain protested good-naturedly.

There was a flash. "Thanks. We're way ahead of you, captain. You can buy a picture of the building down on the avenue for two cents right now. Any of the papers. Including all the news about the big mystery."

"And all the police theories too, I suppose."

"Sure. Why not?"

The captain grinned and strode on. They got into the police car at the curb. They drove down to a restaurant on Farragut Avenue and the captain put in an order for food to be sent up to Chatham House for Bloomingdale and the two officers.

"We ought to have something to eat ourselves," Ingram suggested.

"Good idea," the captain agreed.

They ordered sandwiches and coffee. "Just what," Ingram asked over the food, "is your theory in the case, captain?"

The captain swallowed half a cup of coffee and looked at Ingram with his keen blue eyes.

"I've any number," he replied. "Look at the possibilities. Luciano, Crane, the janitor, Professor Bailey. Your guess is as good as mine. Give me till we've seen Crane and Bailey. Then I'll venture a single theory. And what theory do you have, professor?"

"I haven't any. Only confusion."

"You wouldn't, of course," said the captain, "be keeping anything from us—for the sake of a great university's reputation?" He echoed President Meade's words with pointed directness.

Ingram frowned. "No," he said.

The captain continued amiably: "This university is a wonderful institution, and I suppose you people can hardly be blamed for wanting to keep its name as clean as possible. Somehow or other, professor, I can't get out of my mind your own private little investigation—that is, President Meade's—before you called us in. That sort of thing's a little irregular, you know, and you can't blame me much if I wonder about it. You didn't cover anything up, did you; anything we ought to know?"

"President Meade's sole idea," Ingram replied, "was exactly what he said it was. He wanted, if possible, to get at the truth himself and have the whole thing over with quickly. He had no ulterior motive, I am sure."

"And he didn't cover anything up?"

"Nothing."

They finished their food and left the restaurant. They drove back to Paisley Road, past Chatham House, on through the gloomy darkness to Aldrich Road and from here turned into Price Street, where Ingram pointed out Bailey's house.

They went up the dark path and stood waiting at the door when Ingram had rung the bell. Shortly the door opened and Mary Bailey stood there.

"Good evening," she greeted. "Come in." They walked in. "Ben, why didn't you tell me before about the terrible thing that happened?"

"I couldn't then," Ingram replied. "This is Captain Packer of the homicide squad. This is Miss Bailey. Is your father here, Mary?"

"Yes—upstairs in his study."

"Will you tell him we're here?"

"Yes." She went upstairs and returned in a few moments. "Go right up," she said. The captain started up the stairs. Mary caught hold of Ben Ingram's sleeve and halted him. "Who did this terrible thing, Ben? Do they know?"

"No," Ingram replied. "They don't know." He drew away and joined the captain on the stairs.

Professor Bailey was sitting at his desk. The only light in the room was the desk lamp. He got up as these two entered. Ingram introduced them. Professor Bailey drew up a chair for the captain and Ingram seated himself back in the shadows where he could watch both the captain and Bailey.

"Pretty serious business, this," the captain said. "I wondered, Professor Bailey, if you could give us any help."

"I'll do anything I can," Bailey assured him. It seemed to Ingram that he had regained the poise he had lost earlier in the evening.

"Tell me, professor," Packer asked, "have you been to Chatham House today?"

"No," Bailey replied. "I rarely go there on Wednesdays."

"Did you go over in that direction at all this afternoon?"

"I went for a short walk," Bailey replied, "down Paisley Road and back again."

"When was that?"

"About two-thirty. I'm not sure of the time."

"How far did you go?"

"Down to Farragut Avenue."

"You didn't turn in at the little lane there in front of Chatham House, did you?"

"No, I didn't. We strolled down to the avenue and back."

"We? Who else?"

"Professor Davis and I."

"Is Professor Davis a member of the English Department, too? Does he have an office in Chatham House?"

"Yes."

"Did he stop in there during your stroll?"

"No. We were together all the time."

"Did you see anybody going toward or away from Chatham House?"

"I took no notice. We were talking and I didn't pay any attention to persons that might have been nearby."

The captain asked: "What were you talking about, professor?"

Bailey hesitated. "I—I don't recall at the moment. We were just chatting—"

The captain leaned forward. "You were so intent on what you were chatting about that you didn't notice if persons were nearby, and yet you can't recall what you were discussing? Come now, professor. Try to remember."

A strained expression had come now to Bailey's face. He licked dry lips and attempted to play the part of a man remembering something that has slipped from his mind. It was clear to Ingram that Bailey and Davis had neglected to go into this detail. Bailey would tell one story, Davis another, and Captain Packer would jump at the irresistible conclusion of a poorly-patched alibi.

"I—ah—strange, I don't seem to remember," Bailey said lamely. He was nervous now. Ingram saw it and knew that Captain Packer saw it as well.

The captain pressed the point, his voice, Ingram thought, a little harder: "Surely, professor, you can remember some little scrap of the conversation you had."

"I—I have a very poor memory," Bailey explained. "Things slip my mind. The absent-minded professor, you know." He laughed hollowly. "Let me see. I think we talked about things in the English Department. That's it. Yes. Things in the English Department."

Captain Packer nodded. His eyes did not leave Bailey for a moment.

"Professor," he said, going abruptly off on a new tack, "you sent us permission, by Professor Ingram, to open your theme box by force. He said you had lost your key to it. When did you lose it, professor?"

"I haven't had it since yesterday."

"I see. Now—about this student of yours—Guido Luciano. He was given extra time on a theme. Is that so?"

"Yes. That's right."

Packer was silent for a few moments. "When did you first notice that your key was missing?" he asked.

"Last night—when I emptied the pockets of the suit I was wearing."

"Have you any idea where you lost it?"

"None. I don't keep it on my key ring. And it was a small key—easily misplaced. I haven't the faintest idea what has happened to it."

"And you haven't a duplicate?"

"No. I did have another some months ago. I lost that too."

"Awkward," the captain remarked. "If you lose them so easily, you ought to keep several duplicates."

"I've meant to have some made but never got round to it."

"Hm.  . . . Professor, about an hour ago I forced open your theme box, looking for Luciano's theme. Luciano says he put it in at three o'clock. I found the box empty. Who do you suppose, professor, took that theme out of the box?"

Bailey shrugged. "The one, I suppose, who either found or stole my key."

"But why should anyone go to the trouble of stealing a— theme paper?"

"I don't know." Bailey moved uneasily. He was losing his poise again. To Ingram he looked terribly old, ill. The captain was unmistakably suspicious; he tapped the arm of his chair ruminatively, then said to Bailey:

"I'd like to have you come along with me, professor. I want you to tell your story to the district attorney. He's down at Chatham House. Will you get your hat, please?"

"Is that necessary?" Bailey asked. "I've told you all I know."

"Why," the captain inquired dryly, "should you mind telling it again?"

Bailey got up stiffly. "Very well. I'll go along with you. I'll get my hat."

His face was haggard, his step along the carpet slow. His head, usually erect, was bowed. He went out, closed the door. The captain said nothing, nor did Ingram.

In a few moments there was a knock at the door.

"Come in," Ingram called. The door opened and Mary Bailey stood there. She came in and closed the door.

"Ben," she said, "tell me what's the trouble. Father came out of here looking simply ghastly. Tell me what's happened."

Ingram said: "Nothing, Mary. Nothing at all. The captain has just been asking your father a few questions."

Mary faced the captain. "Asking my father a few questions about Professor Yerkes's murder! And why should you ask him questions? You can't be so idiotic as to believe he knows anything about it, captain!"

"Mary!" Ingram interposed quickly. "It isn't that. The captain merely wants to know if your father can help us any. You don't understand. You don't know the details."

"I do know, however, that what you've said to him has upset him—upset him horribly, captain."

The captain murmured: "I'm sorry, miss."

Mary turned away now without a glance at Ben Ingram. She went out, closed the door. The captain faced Ingram, raising his eyebrows. Ingram said nothing. In silence they awaited Bailey's return.

Suddenly there was a scream. It was Mary. Ingram ran to the door, threw it open.

"Ben!" She was calling from the other end of the house. "Oh, Ben! Come; hurry! It's Father! Oh, Dad! Dad! Daddy darling!"

Ingram ran down the hallway to Professor Bailey's bedroom. The door was open. Mary was bending over her father, who lay sprawled in a great armchair. Mary turned to them, frantic with fear. She had a small bottle in her hand.

"Ben!" she gasped. "Ben!" She held out the bottle. The captain got to it first and took it from her.

"Poison!" he snapped. "Quick, Ingram, call a doctor. And you, miss, show me the kitchen—in a hurry! I'll mix him an antidote. Come—don't stand there—if you want your father to live!"

# 10
## WEDNESDAY 9 P.M.

Half an hour later Professor Bailey was out of danger.

"But you mustn't talk to him, captain," Dr. Royal warned. "I won't have it. He's in no condition for it. Probably won't be for days. He's to stay in bed and have quiet."

"All right," said Packer, "but there'll be an officer here in the house—just to see that nothing more happens."

"Suit yourself," said the doctor irritably. "I don't agree that this was attempted suicide. He went into the bathroom for a sedative. In his agitation he took it in the dark."

"And it turned out not to be a sedative," the captain remarked dryly.

"It's happened before," Royal snapped.

Bloomingdale, who had come over in a hurry from Chatham House, was pacing the floor of the library with long strides, listening silently to the exchange of opinions between the doctor and Captain Packer. He had not yet had an opportunity to discuss the matter with Packer. Now, at length, the doctor went to the door.

"I'm going to have another look at him, then I'll be running along. Please be gentle with him."

"I'll do my best," said Packer. Bloomingdale followed Dr. Royal to the door and closed it behind him.

"Well, what's the story?" he asked Packer. "The details."

"It's some kind of a lead," Packer said, lowering his voice. "I'm not sure just what kind."

"How'd it come about?"

"Well, I came over with Ingram. The girl, Mary Bailey, let us in. We went upstairs to see the professor. He was nervous when I questioned him. Struck me as covering up something. He was afraid of the questioning—no doubt about that. And then, when I asked him to come along and have a chat with you—well, he went out to get his hat—and took poison."

"And when you brought him around he said he'd taken it by mistake?"

The captain swore. "No! It was that doctor—Dr. Royal. He put the words in his mouth. Told him he must have taken it by mistake. So what does Bailey do but agree with him."

Bloomingdale sat down. "Well, we'll have another go at him when he's feeling better. Nothing to do but wait. By the way, tell me what you think about Ingram."

The captain shrugged. "Seems all right. Good enough feller. Fond of this Mary Bailey and, for that reason, I think we'll get no help from him of any kind—if it involves Bailey. . . . Say! What about this angle—his finding Yerkes? It makes the neatest theory in the world that he came in there, killed Yerkes, then reported it."

"What about the voices Luciano heard—talking with Yerkes before Ingram got there?" Bloomingdale asked.

"Oh, yes," said Packer. "I'd forgotten that for a moment."

"Your best angle right now," Bloomingdale stated, "is the Bailey-Davis one. Why don't you drop in on Davis? I'll go back and see if Crane or the janitor have come in. They're my hunch. They'll know something—those people—and when we get hold of them, I believe we'll be able to do something besides guess."

There was a knock at the door. Packer opened it. It was Ingram.

"May I come in?" he asked.

"Do," Bloomingdale said.

Ingram entered, closed the door. "Tell me," he began, "what are you going to do about Professor Bailey?"

Bloomingdale shrugged. "There isn't much to do until he's fit to talk again. We'll wait and then—"

"Do you or don't you believe he took that poison by accident?"

Bloomingdale showed empty hands. "Your guess is as good as mine."

Ingram said nothing.

"Well," Bloomingdale declared, "I've got to get back to Chatham House. See you later, captain."

"Mind if I go along?" Ingram inquired. "I want to get some things from my desk."

"Come along."

They went out into the hallway. Mary Bailey met them there. Bloomingdale went on ahead. Ingram halted for a few moments.

"Ben," Mary said, her hand upon his, "I want you to know that I'd be frightened beyond words if it weren't for you."

Ingram caressed her hand gently. "Count on me," he said, then went away after Bloomingdale.

They drove to Chatham House. Ingram, silent, floundered in a hopeless, bottomless gloom. Why, he queried, should Bailey take poison if not that he feared the police would force his secret from him? It looked as if he preferred death to discovery. Ingram did not believe that the poison had been a mistake.

They drew up beside Chatham House and pushed their way through the crowds of students and reporters. Caffrey opened at Bloomingdale's knock.

"Has Crane come in yet?" Bloomingdale wanted to know.

"Not yet."

"The janitor?"

"No, sir."

Bloomingdale went across the corridor to Ingram's office. He threw his hat on the desk, picked up the telephone and called President Meade's home.

"Dr. Meade," he said, "I want authority to open all the theme boxes here. If I can't have the keys right away, I want to force them. Can you give me that authority?"

The president said: "It would probably take some time to get all the keys for you. I think that, if you feel it's absolutely necessary, you may force them. I'll take the responsibility. Has anything further happened?"

Meade knew nothing of the poison episode.

"No," Bloomingdale lied, "nothing."

"Let me hear of any progress."

"Of course. Thanks, doctor." Bloomingdale hung up, picked up Ingram's bronze paper knife and strode out into the corridor.

There were eight boxes besides Professor Bailey's. Bloomingdale opened them all. Some were empty, others contained papers. Bloomingdale examined each paper and dropped them all back into their boxes.

"Well, it didn't get into any of these other boxes by mistake," he said to Ingram.

They went back to Ingram's office and sat down for a smoke. The district attorney sat with wrinkled brow, absorbed in thought.

After a while Captain Packer came in. He shook his head at Bloomingdale's questioning glance.

"Blind alley," he grumbled. "What do you suppose Davis said when I asked him what he and Bailey chatted about coming down Paisley Road?"

"Matters in the English Department?" Bloomingdale ventured.

"Right. Even gave me details. That's where I slipped up. What could have been easier than for Bailey to phone Davis when he left us in his study there? There are several phones in the house—extensions."

"And then," Ingram suggested with faint bitterness, "he felt so good at having put one over on you, he went and mixed himself a poison cocktail."

Packer looked soberly at Ingram. "No. Went and mixed himself a sedative. You wouldn't believe anything against Bailey, would you, professor?"

"I know him too well to believe anything like this against him."

To Bloomingdale Packer said: "I suppose there's no word of Crane or the janitor?"

"None."

Packer decided thoughtfully: "I'd like to get into that janitor's place downstairs—to see if we could find anything indicating flight."

Bloomingdale reached for the telephone. "I'll call Meade again and see if we can have keys or authority to force and enter. By the way, I forced the other theme boxes out there. Not a sign of The Movement to Abolish the Death Penalty."

He got the president on the wire again.

"If you must, you must," Meade said wearily. "Yes, yes. Force the door. You might call the head janitor's place first to see if he has a key."

But the head janitor had no key to Schultz's quarters. "If the president says bust in, bust in," he told Bloomingdale. "That's good enough authority, ain't it?"

"It is," Bloomingdale agreed, and hung up. He rose. "Let's go downstairs, captain, and have a look."

Ingram remained seated. He had no intention of prowling about after these men. Deep in somber thought about Bailey he remained in his office, wondering, doubting, utterly confused. . . .

Packer led the way down the basement stairs. Halfway along the dimlit passage, at the rear door, sat Murphy on a chair without a back. He got up.

"How's the weather down here?" Packer asked.

"All clear, captain. Not a sign of anything. Only noises."

They halted. "What kind of noises?" Bloomingdale asked.

"Mice. Rats. And now and then I hear something breathing."

"Breathing!" Packer echoed. "What did you hear breathing?"

"Don't know. It gave me the jumps when I heard it first. It would go on for a little while, then it would stop. I haven't heard it now for ten, fifteen minutes."

Packer and Bloomingdale stood listening now. A hush fell in the passage. There came, in a few moments, the sound of tiny scurrying feet, abrupt rustlings, and then began a slow, purposeful gnawing sound.

"That feller," Murphy muttered, "has been gnawing for an hour."

"You don't hear the breathing now, do you?" Packer asked.

"Not now. No, it wasn't any imagination, captain. I tell you, I heard breathing."

"What kind of breathing?"

"Well, a sort of heavy breathing, like an animal asleep."

"Like an animal! What kind of an animal?"

"I—well, I don't know."

"Where was it coming from?"

Murphy's brow wrinkled. "I couldn't tell that. I thought it was from one of these bins here. I went up and down and listened at each of 'em, but I couldn't seem to place it."

"It wasn't—" Captain Packer pointed suddenly down the corridor. "It wasn't from that door, was it? The janitor's place?"

"I don't think so. I listened there. Besides, there's no one in there, is there?"

Packer went down to the end of the corridor and stood before the janitor's door. There was a single wooden step up to the threshold. On this the captain stood, listening intently. After a few seconds he pressed his ear close to the door panel.

Bloomingdale was beside him now. "Anything there?" he queried.

"Nothing. Wait! Now there's something. No. You give it a listen."

Bloomingdale put his ear to the door. There was a hush in the passage now. Suddenly Murphy started forward and said in an undertone: "There! There it is now! You hear it? Where's it coming from?"

"It's coming," Bloomingdale declared, "from behind this door."

"And it's no more the sound of an animal," Packer said, "than it is of an airplane. It's a man sleeping. Let me at it, Mr. Bloomingdale."

He thumped on the panel with the side of his great fist.

"Hullo, there!" he cried. "Who's in there? Wake up! Open the door! In the name of the Law, open this door!"

They listened again. The sound of the breathing was quite distinct now.

There was no answer to the captain's command. The breathing went on.

"All right," Bloomingdale ordered. "Break it down."

# 11
## WEDNESDAY 10 P.M.

The captain stepped back and drove at the door with shoulder and hip. There was a crash and the sound of wood ripped apart, and the captain fell into the darkness beyond the door. The door struck a wall behind it and bounded back crazily. Bloomingdale stayed it with his foot. Packer got up, dusting his hands.

Bloomingdale peered past him into the shadows. It seemed to be a long, narrow room. The captain thrust his hand into a pocket for a small electric torch and turned its light down the length of the room. A worn, faded brown rug covered the floor. There was an old rickety armchair, a battered desk covered with papers. On the right, in the far corner, was a bed, and on the bed lay a man.

He was on his back, arms at his side. He wore shoes, dirty brown shoes. His clothes were old, soiled. He wore a vest which did not match the trousers, and his coat, which matched neither trousers nor vest, was on the floor beside the bed. The face, coarse, heavy-featured, bore a stubble of reddish beard. The lips, relaxed, open slightly, were thick and pale. The face was white, tinted with a faint, unhealthy yellow. He was nearly bald, with a border of thick red-brown hair at the sides, and straggling wisps lying across the bald spot.

The air in the room was stuffy, dead. The captain sniffed and made a face. Two windows, which looked out on a level with the ground at the rear of the building, were closed.

Packer shone the light on the sleeper's face, laid a hand on his shoulder and shook him.

"Wake up!" said he. But the man slept on. Packer shook him again, this time more vigorously. "Wake up, you!" He handed the light to Bloomingdale, took the man by both shoulders now, raised him to a sitting position and shook him once more. He was limp as a sack of flour. His eyes remained closed. Packer laid him back again.

"That's no natural sleep," he said. "This gentleman's drugged."

Bloomingdale stooped suddenly and picked up a small bottle from under the edge of the bed. It was empty, without a cork.

"Right you are. Sleeping potion. Look. Every bit of it's gone." He stepped across the narrow room to a wash basin in a corner. He turned again to Packer, holding out a tumbler. "He took it in this. See the white particles at the bottom and on the sides?"

Captain Packer grunted. "He's Schultz the janitor, I suppose. And this is where he's been while we've been waiting for him."

"Let's check up," Bloomingdale said. "Murphy, ask Professor Ingram to come down, will you?"

Murphy went off down the corridor. Bloomingdale discovered a light cord over his head and pulled it. A small bulb on the end of a wire that dangled from the ceiling, threw out a weak light. The bulb swayed back and forth and the light cast shadows grotesquely along the floor and sent them climbing the walls and springing back again.

The room was dingy, dirty; everything in it was shabby and sad-looking. Packer glanced about him. Bloomingdale stood contemplating the face of the sleeping man.

"Now why," Packer queried, "should he take a sleeping potion right at a time like this?"

There was the sound of footsteps on the stairway. Then Ingram came down the passage, followed by Murphy. At the door Ingram halted.

"Come in, Ingram," Bloomingdale said. "Tell us, who's this chap?"

Ingram walked in. He stood looking at the sleeping man with a puzzled glance. "Why, that's Schultz, the janitor of the building," he stated. "What's the matter with him?"

"Drugged. Took a sleep inducer, and plenty of it, too."

"You found him here like that?"

"Yes."

"Then he's been here all the time?"

"Can't say. We'll need a doctor to wake him. Will you get Dr. Royal, or shall I call Thayer?"

"Royal will come. I'll phone him." He stood at the bedside. "This is very strange."

"Might mean any one of several things—don't you think, professor?"

"I don't understand what it means," Ingram replied. "You've tried to wake him, of course?"

"Yes, but he's too far gone. He needs something to counteract the effect of the drug he took."

Ingram went to the door. "I'll call Dr. Royal," he said and strode off down the passage.

Dr. Royal came fifteen minutes later. He took a look at the bottle that had contained the hypnotic and handed it back to the district attorney.

"What we want, doctor," Bloomingdale said, "is to talk with this fellow as soon as possible. Can he be brought out of it in a hurry?"

"Probably not in a hurry," the doctor said, "and I'm not sure how long he'll stay out of it. I think I can bring him back, though, if you insist."

"Will he be able to understand and answer questions?"

"He'll be pretty stupid."

The doctor administered a stimulant by mouth, then held a small bottle of aromatic spirits of ammonia under Schultz's nose. The man stirred and turned his face away.

"There he comes," Packer murmured.

"Open a window," said the doctor. "The air in here is foul. He'll need plenty of fresh air. Don't believe I could stay awake long here myself."

The eyelids of the sleeping man flickered and the eyes opened drowsily. He raised a hand and tried to push away the doctor's hand from beneath his nose. He muttered something under his breath.

"Go 'way," he grumbled. "Go 'way."

The doctor handed the bottle to Captain Packer. "Here," he said, "keep at him with that. Don't suffocate him with it, though. I'll boil up some water and give him a shot of strychnine. It'll probably speed him up. Slap his face a bit if you want—but don't double up your fist, captain, will you?"

The captain sat down beside Schultz and applied the ammonia fumes. The doctor took his bag and went into the back room that led off the bedroom. It was a tiny kitchen. The doctor found a clean enamel dish, poured some water into it, set it on the small gas stove to boil and placed the parts of a hypodermic needle in it. Ingram came into the kitchen and stood beside him.

"They got anything on Schultz?" Dr. Royal asked softly.

"I don't know," Ingram replied in an undertone.

For several minutes the hypodermic lay in the boiling water. Schultz was protesting feebly at the captain's efforts to rouse him. The doctor put the needle together, loaded it and took the captain's place at the bedside. Schultz lay muttering, eyes closed.

"He's awake," the captain said. "Awake enough to do a bit of swearing. He's been telling me where to go for five minutes."

The doctor sterilized a spot on Schultz's arm. "Steady now, Schultz," he said. "Here's the needle." He jabbed it in and the janitor winced. His eyes opened quickly, then closed again. The doctor shot in the solution and Schultz bit his lip. "He's with us all right," the doctor said, "and this'll bring him around so you can chat with him." He got up now.

The captain took his place, waiting in silence for about a minute, then, at a nod from the doctor, he said: "Come on, now, Schultz, you'll have to talk sooner or later. Open your eyes, if you can, and pay attention." Schultz remained motionless, eyes still closed.

"You're through playing possum," the captain went on. "Better open up and tell us why you killed Professor Yerkes."

The eyes opened this time in alarm. They did not close again. They remained fixed, filled with shock and horror, upon the captain.

The janitor gasped, gulped, licked leathery lips with a dry tongue. "I dunno," he protested weakly, "what you're talkin' about!"

"Why'd you kill Yerkes?" the captain demanded. "You killed him, didn't you?—and then came down here and doped yourself! Did you think that would get you out of it? Who do you think you're fooling?"

"I dunno—what—you're talkin'—about," Schultz muttered drowsily now. "I never killed—nobody. I dunno. I dunno—what you're talkin' about."

"Well, what was your reason for taking that sleeping medicine—a bottleful? What was the reason? Come on! Talk!"

"I dunno. I was—sick. Wanted to sleep. Couldn't sleep. I—"

His head lowered, the eyes closed as if weighted. He was asleep again. The captain shook him. Schultz wakened once more.

"Lemme alone," he begged. "Lemme sleep." His eyes closed.

The captain looked up at Dr. Royal. "Is he bluffing, doctor?"

"Probably not."

The captain stood up, glanced at Bloomingdale. The latter shrugged. "We'll have to wait, I suppose," he said. "When will he be fit, doctor?"

"Probably by tomorrow morning."

"Very well," said Bloomingdale. "Tomorrow morning it is. But the next thing to do—and right away—is to get that head janitor's pass key. I want every office in this place opened. We'll see if we have any more sleeping beauties around this place." He started out of the janitor's quarters. "Coming, Ingram?"

Behind him, puzzled, slow of pace, came Ben Ingram.

## 12
## WEDNESDAY 10:45 P.M.

In his office Ingram glanced at his watch, stifled a yawn.

Bloomingdale said: "You've had a hard day, professor. You ought to go home and get some rest."

"Good idea. I'm dog tired. You're welcome to the office as long as you need it. Want the key?"

"Not necessary. I'll leave it unlatched, if that's all right. By the way—before you go—tell me a little more about Yerkes. Did he have any kin hereabouts?"

"None that I know about."

"Where did he live?"

"Over on Green Street. He had a small house there—one that he rented from the university."

"Who lived there with him?"

"His housekeeper. An old lady—probably seventy."

"I see. Thanks. That's all for now, professor."

"Very well. Good night. Good night, captain."

They echoed his farewell. Ingram went gratefully out into the cool air of Chatham Lane, out of the gloom of Chatham House. The place would never be the same again. Yerkes would haunt it forever. Poor old Yerkes. . . .

The reporters had vanished from their gathering place before the door and so had the students. But, as Ingram reached Paisley Road he saw several cars there and dark heads nodding in conversation and the glow of cigarettes. Students and reporters waiting for scraps of news; news that was being so carefully censored.

Ingram walked north on Paisley Road. He would go up to
Professor Bailey's and see how Bailey was and learn if Mary was
all right. He strolled slowly in the dark. There was a misted moon
overhead and a damp chill in the air now. He thrust his hands
into his trousers pockets and hunched his shoulders against the
chill.

At the Bailey home, Mary answered his ring.

"Come in, Ben. Please come in and talk to me. I'm so confused. I don't know where I am in all this. I don't understand it."

"I don't either," he told her.

She drew him into the sitting room. "Tell me," she begged,
"what are they saying about Father? Why have they sent a policeman here to stand outside his door? Are they going to accuse
him? Do they think he had anything to do with the murder? It's
so absurd, Ben, and yet so terrible."

"I know. You see, Mary, it's simply that they're as confused as
you and I are. They haven't anything against your father. They
simply aren't willing to believe that he took the poison by mistake."

She sat down wearily. "That means that they think he wanted
to die because he—"

"Don't say it. It isn't true. Your father wouldn't hurt any one.
You know that. I tell you, they have nothing—no evidence of any
kind against him. If they've put an officer here, it's merely to see
that no harm comes to him."

"You think so?" she queried with a deep breath of relief. "Do
you really think that? And they've nothing—no suspicion of him?"

"I think it would be better to say," Ingram told her, "that they
suspect everybody. They do—including me. We're all unknown
quantities to them and they must scrutinize us all carefully. I
wonder," he said after a pause, "if I might go up and talk with
your father for a few minutes. Do you think it would be all
right?"

"I think so. If you'll promise not to stay too long and not say
anything to upset him."

"What about the policeman? Will he let me talk with him
alone?"

"I believe so. I've been in there with him alone."

Ingram went upstairs. "I want to see Professor Bailey," he said to the officer at the door.

"Go ahead," was the reply. "He's not under arrest."

Professor Bailey lay in his bed and opened his eyes as Ingram entered. Ingram sat down in a chair beside the bed.

"Uncle Hardy," he began softly, "I've come to tell you that if there's anything I can do to help you, I want to do it."

A faint smile stirred Bailey's lips. "That's very good of you, Ben. I don't know of anything you can do." He closed his eyes once more and in a little while opened them again. "Yes, there is something."

"What is it?"

"See that nothing happens to Mary while I'm here like this. Will you do that?"

"I will indeed. You know that I will."

"Thank you, Ben. You're a good lad. You always were."

His eyes were heavy. Ingram laid a hand on his shoulder. "Better try to sleep," he said, getting up. Bailey smiled faintly again. Ingram tiptoed out.

The officer at the door asked: "How's he doing?"

"He's asleep." Ingram went downstairs. Mary was waiting. "Don't worry about him," Ingram advised. "He's doing very well. He needs rest now, more than anything else."

He bade her good night. "Phone me at once," he said, "if you need me. Promise."

"I promise."

Ingram walked home wearily. The strain of the long day was upon him. His worries increased and deepened. He feared what the truth must bring to Bailey and Davis. He feared desperately for them. . . .

He went to bed and lay awake for a long time, staring at the dark ceiling, studying the problem from all angles, getting nowhere. Perhaps, he told himself at length, they would know more when the student Crane showed up, or when Schultz talked. But what, then, would they know? He dreaded the denouement that must come, feared the morrow with a torturing, gnawing fear.

At last he fell asleep. It was an interminable night of bad dreams that seemed to go on forever.

There was a knock at his door. He wakened with a start.

"Come in," he called.

It was Mrs. Eagan, his housekeeper.

"There's a gentleman downstairs to see you, professor," she told him. "His name is Captain Packer. He said he's from the police and wanted I should wake you. He wants to see you at once, he says."

"Tell him to come up." Ingram yawned, rubbed his eyes. Mrs. Eagan went out. Ingram got out of bed, donned robe and slippers and heard Packer's step outside in the hall as he went to the dresser to brush down his tousled hair.

"Come in, captain."

The door opened. Captain Packer walked in. "Good morning," he said gravely. His heavy, square face looked pinched with fatigue.

Ingram glanced at his watch. It was seven o'clock. "What's the news so early?" he asked.

The captain sat down on the bed. "Look here, professor," he said, "you say you knew Yerkes about as well as anybody hereabouts. If you did, can't you give us a little more information about his contacts? Who he went about with, especially in the last six months or so; who he avoided; what he thought of the various people about him?"

Ingram told him: "Yerkes talked very little. He was, as I have told you, a kind of hermit. Almost always alone. When one was with him, he said little. He was a preoccupied, taciturn man."

The captain passed a hand over his brow. His mouth was set grimly. "You can't say how well he knew the student named Crane, or if he had had much to do with him lately? Or if they had anything in common?"

"In common?" Ingram echoed. "Has Crane turned up for questioning?"

"Yes and no," the captain answered. "He's turned up, but not for questioning."

Startled, Ingram met the captain's eyes quickly. "What do you mean?"

"I mean," the captain informed him, "that Crane was found dead in the bushes in your so-called North Park just about an hour ago. He was shot clean through the heart. He was shot last night. He was dead probably all the while we were looking for him."

# 13
## THURSDAY 7 A.M.

Scarcely able to believe, Ingram stared in horror.

"Crane!" he exclaimed. "In heaven's name, captain, what does all this mean?"

"That," the captain returned, "is what I want to talk with you about. You see, professor, last night one of our theories was that Crane was possibly the murderer of Professor Yerkes. It wasn't an unreasonable theory, under the circumstances. But now he's dead, and the new theory that stares us in the face is that he knew something vital about the murder of Yerkes and was put out of the way for that reason."

Ingram nodded slowly. The captain went on:

"Now, professor, you were one of the three who spoke with Crane. Your Dr. Royal is a little too much on his dignity to talk frankly with. Besides being touchy on the honor of the university, he doesn't trust policemen very much. Not that I blame him. Your president, of course, would probably be thinking so much about suppressing the news in the papers that he wouldn't be able to give it without easing up on details. And after seeing last night's papers and this morning's and getting the fresh news of Crane's death, he'd be impossible. So I'm turning to you. I'm asking you to go back over things in your mind and try to pick up any little details you may have forgotten to tell—especially details about Crane."

Ingram sat down in his armchair by the window.

"I'm quite sure," he said, "that I've told you all there was to tell about Crane—all that I know."

"I know. But suppose you go over the story about him again—his coming to see you people just after Yerkes's death."

"It was President Meade who told you about that. I'm quite sure he gave you the story exactly as it happened."

"I'm sure he did. I was just hoping that you might have something to add—your interpretation of Crane's actions—his excitement under the questioning, his fainting. How did you interpret it at the time, professor?"

"At the time," Ingram replied, "I was inclined to make no judgment against the boy. He was badly upset, but the circumstances and the mode of questioning were sufficient alone to have upset him so. However, considering what has happened since, I can readily see that his actions were caused by fear of what he might be forced to tell."

The captain looked troubled, confounded. "You see what's happened," he complained, "because your good Dr. Meade wouldn't call in the police? If we had talked with Crane first and his actions had been suspicious, we'd have taken steps to see that nothing happened to him until he decided to tell the truth. . . . It's no good, though, to cry over spilt milk."

There was a silence. Then, his thoughts returning to Yerkes, Ingram asked: "Have you been to Yerkes's home and talked with his housekeeper?"

"Yes. There was nothing to learn there. His next of kin is some distant relative living heaven knows where. And from what the old lady says, Yerkes had very little to leave to any one. All those angles seem to be no good."

The telephone at Ingram's bedside rang. Ingram answered it, handed the instrument to Packer.

"It's Bloomingdale," he announced. "Wants to talk to you."

Half a minute later the captain hung up and said: "Our friend Schultz is awake." He picked up his hat.

"Sorry I couldn't offer anything that would help," Ingram said.

"Never mind. Sorry I got you out of bed so early. Good morning, professor."

"Good morning."

Ingram bathed, shaved and dressed in the deepest thought. At breakfast he read the morning paper with its account of Yerkes's killing and the columns of hearsay. Finished with his meal, he went out to the garage and drove out his car.

Halfway down Aldrich Road, along North Park, he saw a number of students. He parked his car, walked down a narrow path into the park and went along to join the little knot of men and women gathered in the path. He saw the blue of an officer's uniform.

Ingram joined the group. One of the students was telling the others what had happened. He pointed to a spot where the bushes were broken.

"I guess he was shot at the edge of the gravel walk and then shoved into the bushes out of sight," he explained.

"Didn't anybody hear the shot?" someone asked.

"I guess not. Maybe no one was near enough. Or perhaps, if any one did hear it, they thought it was an automobile backfiring. It's pretty hard to tell a shot from a backfire sometimes."

"I suppose so."

Ingram stood watching and listening for a few minutes, then returned to his car. He sat at the wheel, pondering these things.

What did Schultz know? What would the police learn from him?

In a few minutes Ingram started his car and drove off to Chatham House, and on the way students stopped and turned to stare after him.

# 14
## THURSDAY 7:30 A.M.

Bloomingdale led the way downstairs. At the door of Schultz's room, which was open, stood a uniformed officer who had relieved Murphy.

Behind Bloomingdale came Packer, Johnny Mortimer, an assistant district attorney, and a stenographer. Bloomingdale went in and stood at the foot of Schultz's bed. Schultz lay with his face to the wall, grumbling unintelligible words.

"Come now, Schultz," Bloomingdale began, "we're going to have a little talk. Turn around here and sit up."

Schultz twisted round on to his back and looked up at Bloomingdale with bleared eyes.

"I'm a sick man," he whined. "Go 'way and lemme alone."

"We'll let you alone as soon as we've had a talk. If you're sick, you ought to go to a hospital. This is no place for a sick man."

"I'll go any place I want!" Schultz protested. "I'll stay here if I want."

"Suit yourself. Come now, sit up."

Grumbling, eyeing with suspicion the men who stood behind the district attorney, Schultz raised himself to a sitting position. His puffy, unshaven face was sullen.

"What do you want anyhow?" he demanded in thick, sluggish syllables.

Bloomingdale seated himself on the edge of the bed. The stenographer flipped open a notebook, put a pencil behind his ear and took another from his pocket. Mortimer and Packer stood at the foot of the bed.

"Do you know who we are?" Bloomingdale asked.

"The police, I guess."

"I'm the district attorney. That is Captain Packer of the homicide squad. Do you know why we're here?"

"No. I don't know nothin'."

"We spoke with you last night. Do you remember that?"

"No."

"Probably you don't. You weren't very wide awake. All right. We'll start again. Listen carefully. Yesterday afternoon, at about three o'clock, Professor Yerkes was murdered in his office upstairs. I want to know two things from you, Schultz. Where were you at that time—and what do you know about the professor's death?"

Schultz said: "I don't know nothin'. I didn't even know he was dead. I don't know nothin'. I'm a sick man. I wanna be left alone."

"Where were you at three o'clock, yesterday afternoon?"

"I was right here. I was right here in bed. I was sleepin'."

"Exactly when was it you came in here and went to sleep?"

"I dunno."

"Don't know! Was it yesterday morning? Was it day before yesterday? Was it last week? Come now—talk up!"

"I guess it was yesterday mornin'."

"What time?"

"About eleven o'clock, I guess."

"At eleven o'clock you came in here, took that sleeping potion and you've been here ever since? Is that what you want me to believe?"

"Yes."

"Had you ever taken a sleeping potion before?"

"Yes. Lots o' times."

"What's the dose you take? How much of that stuff at a time?"

"It says on the bottle to take what you can put in the bottle cap."

"And that dose makes you sleep how long?"

"I dunno."

"Don't know! Of course you know! The bottle says—doesn't it?—that one dose will help you get a night's sleep. You slept from eleven o'clock yesterday morning until an hour ago. That's equal to nearly three nights' sleep. Listen, Schultz! You took more than one dose. You took an overdose. Even the doctor couldn't bring you out of it. Now tell me why you did it. Were you trying to put yourself out of the way—kill yourself?"

"No, sir. No. Why should I kill myself?"

"Well, then, tell me why you took an overdose."

"I—I was sick. I thought I ought to get a lot o' sleep."

"If you were sick, why didn't you go up to the infirmary?"

"I had work to do. I couldn't go up there while I had work to do."

"You couldn't go to the infirmary because you had work to do, but you could take enough dope to lay you out a whole day and night! Now, stop lying, Schultz. You took that dope to provide an alibi for yourself. You went upstairs to Professor Yerkes's office and shot him. You took the dope—"

A look of horror had come into Schultz's eyes. "No, sir! No, sir! I didn't kill him! I never killed nobody!"

"Oh, yes you did! You killed Yerkes! Otherwise you wouldn't have—"

"No, sir, I didn't! I never killed Professor Yerkes!"

"Then what do you know about who did kill him? It's one way or the other. Either you killed him or you know who did! Own up, now! Which is it? Did you do it or are you shielding some one who did? You killed him, didn't you?"

Schultz's voice rose suddenly to a hoarse shout.

"No! I never killed him! I never killed him!"

"Yes, you did—and you'll go to the chair for it!"

"No! You can't send me to the chair. I never killed him! I only know—" He stopped abruptly, and his breath came in sharp, short gasps. He stared, bloodshot eyes wide, at Bloomingdale. He trembled violently and gripped the bedsheet in desperation.

"Oh, you know something, do you?" Bloomingdale pressed him. "Then tell what you know! Out with it! And no more lies! Understand?"

Schultz subsided, licked dry lips with a dry tongue. He nodded dumbly, fearfully.

He said: "I want a drink of water."

"Get him some water," Bloomingdale ordered. Mortimer went to the wash basin, filled a glass and placed it in Schultz's trembling hand. The man spilled half of it on himself and gulped the other half nervously. His Adam's apple bobbed. He set the glass down on the bed and closed his eyes. He bit his lip now and tears came down his cheeks. Burying his face suddenly in his hands, he moaned: "I wish I'd die! I wish I'd die!"

"We're waiting," Bloomingdale said. "Let's have it."

Schultz dried his eyes with red fists. Then he sat looking despondently at his rough fingers. Bloomingdale urged him again. At length he began, as if forcing himself to speak.

"I'm only tellin'," he whined, "because I'm a coward. I'm a yeller-dog coward—that's what I am. That's why I'm tellin'. They been too good to me. I wish I'd died. I wish I'd taken enough dope to die."

"Who are you talking about? Name them."

Schultz said in a voice choked with emotion: "Professor Davis. And Professor Bailey."

Captain Packer gripped the bedpost and leaned forward as Schultz's voice dwindled.

Bloomingdale demanded: "What about Bailey and Davis? What do you know about them?"

Schultz mumbled in a dull voice: "They're the best friends I ever had. I oughta be struck dead for this. I oughta be struck dead."

"Speak up! What happened?"

"Yesterday afternoon," Schultz went on, "I was down here. I was lyin' here asleep and I woke up and heard somebody out there in the cellar passage. I didn't know who it was at first. I was sort o' dizzy from sleepin'—"

"Yes? Go on."

"Well, they stood out there talkin'. I didn't know who it was right away. I got up and went over to the door and I put my ear up against it. Then I heard them say somethin' about Yerkes and somethin' about Yerkes bein' dead. I looked through the keyhole and I seen it was Professor Bailey and Professor Davis."

"You're sure? You're sure it was Bailey and Davis?"

"Yes, sir. I seen 'em. I was lookin' through the keyhole when they went out. When they closed the door I went out there in the passage and I started to go upstairs to see what was what. And just when I got part way up, so I could look over the top o' the stairs and see the first-floor corridor up there, the front door opened. It was Professor Ingram. I saw him come in.

"Then I got scared. I thought maybe if Professor Yerkes was killed and they found me there, I'd get the blame. I got panicky. I came down here and hid in my room. Then, after a time, I sneaked out again and went part way upstairs and listened. I wanted to know if it was honest-to-God truth that Yerkes was killed.

"Then I heard somebody else come in. I could hear Dr. Meade and Dr. Royal. It was both of them, and then I heard Professor Ingram say Professor Yerkes had got murdered.

"I sneaked back again down here. I knew all of a sudden why they sneaked out the back door here. I came back in here and locked the door. After a while someone came down and tried to get in here. It was Professor Ingram. They wanted to ask me about it. I didn't let on I was here. I was scared. I didn't know what to do. So I took a big dose of the sleepin' stuff. And that's all I know."

Bloomingdale said: "And you're absolutely certain you saw Bailey and Davis out there?"

"Yes, sir. God help me—I'm sure."

Bloomingdale stood up. "That'll do for now," he said. To the stenographer: "Transcribe that, read it back and get him to sign. And I want him held, captain, as a material witness. Mortimer, come along upstairs. We'll have a little action now."

He spoke then in an undertone to Packer, stepped out into the corridor and went upstairs, Mortimer at his heels.

He walked into Ingram's office, where Ingram was fumbling idly in a desk drawer.

"Morning, professor. We're getting somewhere at last. Schultz saw Bailey and Davis leave this building by the back door yesterday afternoon, just before you came in. How's that for progress?

Let me at that phone, will you? We'll have a couple of warrants
for those two gentlemen in short order now."

Dumbfounded, Ingram asked: "You're going to arrest Bailey
and Davis for murder?"

"Sure—for murder. Sorry, Ingram. I know how you feel—but
a killer's a killer."

Ingram stared dazedly.

Across the desk he handed Bloomingdale the telephone.

# 15
## THURSDAY 9 A.M.

Professor Bailey was placed under arrest less than an hour later. He was permitted, however, to remain at home in his bed for the time being, with an officer on duty at his door.

Packer himself made the trip to Professor Davis's home. He rang the bell and a maid came to the door.

"Is Professor Davis here?" Packer asked.

"No, sir, but Mrs. Davis is. Would you like to see her?"

"I would. Tell her it's Captain Packer of the police department."

The maid's eyes widened and she hastened away to tell Mrs. Davis. Captain Packer strolled into the living room and stood looking about idly, hands behind his back, a mild frown on his brow.

"How do you do, captain?"

The captain turned to the door and saw a small, frail-looking white-haired woman standing there. She was grave and sweet of face. The captain was impressed at once with the loveliness of her features. Here was a woman who must have been strikingly beautiful when she was young.

"How do you do, ma'am?" Packer said. "I'm Captain Packer. I'm looking for Professor Davis."

"Sit down, please, captain." Mrs. Davis seated herself in a chair by the window and the Captain sat down on the edge of a chair opposite her. She said: "Professor Davis has gone out. Is there anything I can do?"

Packer cleared his throat and said after a brief hesitation: "Well—no, ma'am. My business was with the professor. Can you tell me where he went to?" This, he knew, could be ascertained easily enough in due time, for he had a man following Davis at every step, and he would get a report later. He asked his question almost idly: "Can you tell me where he is? I'd like a word or two with him."

"No," she replied. "He didn't say where he was going. He usually does, but he didn't this time. You know, he's terribly upset about Professor Yerkes. He's hardly himself. He tries to keep it from me—you should see him—but he can't very well. You can't keep those things from a woman, can you, captain?"

"I suppose not," Packer agreed.

"Do they suspect anyone?" Mrs. Davis inquired. "Are the police getting anywhere?"

"Oh, I guess so. We're a little slow, ma'am, but we usually get somewhere in time. The professor didn't say when he was coming back?"

"No, he didn't. But he'll be back for lunch anyhow. You might drop in then. You might come and have lunch with us, captain, if you can spare the time."

Packer looked away from this gentle, unsuspecting soul who would invite to luncheon the man who carried a warrant for her husband's arrest.

"No'm," he refused. "No, thanks. I appreciate it very much; but I'm so busy, I have to grab my food on the run. If you'll excuse me, ma'am."

"Oh, that's all right. I just thought that it would be nicer for you to have your chat with Professor Davis at the table. Is there any place where he can get in touch with you when he comes in? I'll tell him. I'm sure he'll be glad to telephone."

Packer nodded. Glad to telephone. This poor innocent didn't have the faintest idea of what was going on around her. She didn't have the faintest idea that her husband would spend his night in a cell. Packer wondered how she would take the blow when it struck her. He wondered if she was strong enough to stand it. He hated his duty as he glanced momentarily at her serene, gentle face.

He said quietly: "All right, ma'am. You might ask him to give me a ring at that Chatham House. We've sort of set up headquarters there. In Professor Ingram's office. Some one will be there if I'm not and they'll see that the message reaches me." He got up. "I'll go along. If I don't hear from him, I'll drop in again."

She went with him to the door. "Come in any time, captain," she invited. "I'm sure Professor Davis will be glad to help you in any way that he can. Don't hesitate to ask him."

"Thank you. Good day." The captain put on his hat and walked down the driveway. He felt a little foolish. He had come to make an arrest and had remained to feel sorry.

"Ah, damn it!" he said to himself as he strolled down to the car. "I suppose if a man like Davis or one like Bailey let Yerkes have it—well, I suppose he had it coming to him. Who knows?" He shook off these thoughts then. "But who am I to have ideas like this! You weak-minded old fool! The time goes by and you get soft. Twenty—thirty years ago you'd have had no scruples about a thing like this. You'd have hollered at her that you wanted her husband for an old-fashioned murder and you didn't care who knew it. My golly! I should have a woman like that I'd spare on every turn! I wonder would I be a better man and a worse cop or better of both."

And he fell to wondering if it was really his heart gone permanently soft and if he would have been as gentle with any woman, or if it was just that fragile, ethereal, whitehaired soul who made him temporarily this way.

"I wonder," he mused. "She looks as if she had been treated that way all her life. Some people you just can't be unkind to. Ah, me! If you go on like this much more and it leaks out, they'll be asking for your resignation at headquarters. Shake out of it, now."

Moodily he got into the police car beside the driver and said: "Chatham House."

"Isn't he there?" the driver asked. And was amazed when the captain snapped viciously at him: "No, damn it, he isn't! Now, step on it and get me back to Chatham House!"

"Yes, sir," said the driver, and added to himself: "The old boy gets tougher every day. One day he'll get himself a horsewhip and beat us around the place."

# 16
## THURSDAY 9:20 A.M.

On Paisley Road the car drew up beside Chatham House and the captain got out and strode down to the entrance. He paid scant attention to the onlooking students; and to the reporters who asked him what was new he said: "See Bloomingdale."

He went in and found Bloomingdale sitting at Ingram's desk.

"Davis wasn't there," he said and sat down.

"Who's tailing him?" Bloomingdale asked.

"Maguire. No word from him?"

"None. Think Davis has walked out?"

Packer shrugged. "Don't know. Had a little chat with his wife. She invited me to lunch."

Bloomingdale smiled grimly. "I've got some news," he said. "We've picked up Harry Tark—Harry the Dope—one of Corvetti's killers. He had a gun on him—one shot fired. Down at headquarters they say they think it's the gun that killed young Crane. They'll call me as soon as they make sure. They're working on it now."

"Tark—with a gun, with a shot fired? On his person? We never found a gun on him before. He's too smart for that."

"He was doped to the ears, past the smart stage. He was like drunk, they said. Probably too far under to think about getting rid of the gun."

"You think Corvetti's tied up in this?"

"Not necessarily. Tark kills for whoever pays him—Corvetti or anyone else. But I've sent Mortimer down to talk with Corvetti and see what there is to see."

"Hmph! That won't do any good. I know Corvetti. He never knows anything. Why should he? He always wipes his nose off and says it was clean all the time. And go prove something against him. Try it and see how far you get."

"I didn't say I was going to try. I told you Tark kills for anybody's money. But we have to have at least a chat with Corvetti."

"Great feller to have a chat with, too," Packer declared. "He sits you down and gives you a drink and a good cigar and tells you what a good feller he is and you are. And the worst of it is you believe him. I always do."

"So do I. All of which means nothing. Better put a man on Davis's house, to pick him up when he comes in—in case he should lose Maguire."

"I'll do that," Packer said, getting up. "I think—"

The telephone rang. Bloomingdale answered it.

"For you, captain," he said.

"Hello," said Packer into the instrument. "Who is it?"

"Maguire. Has that guy Davis showed up out there? I lost him half an hour ago."

"You what!" Packer roared. "You lost him? What'd you do—stop off for a nap? Listen, Maguire, you pick him up again and—"

"I don't know where he is, captain. I've been looking for him for half an hour. I thought he might have went home."

The captain swore. "You're a hell of a detective, you are! You get in a cab and come over here as fast as you can. And think up a good alibi on the way or I'll have the hide off you!"

"But, captain—"

"Never mind the buts. Come in here with a report—fast!"

He slammed up the receiver. "That dumb dick!" he growled.

"Probably Davis has gone home," Bloomingdale ventured. "I'll call him up."

He put in a call for the Davis home and got Mrs. Davis on the wire.

"This is the district attorney," he said. "Is Professor Davis there—or is he expected?"

"Well—no," Mrs. Davis replied. "I had expected him for lunch, but he called up a few minutes ago and said he wouldn't be able to get here. I don't know where he went. I'm sorry. Shall I have him call you when he gets in?"

"Please," said Bloomingdale.

He hung up and told Packer what Mrs. Davis had said. Packer hunched himself in his chair, lighted a cigar and waited. In ten minutes Maguire came in.

"Well?" Packer demanded. "What happened?"

"Something hot!" Maguire began. "I'm not sure just what it means but—"

"You tell what happened. We'll figure out what it means."

"Well," Maguire said, "this Professor Davis left his house just after I went on duty down there this morning. He walked down to the avenue, took a cab and rode in town. Then he began to walk. He walked over toward the north end and went into a drug store there. He went into a booth and made a call. Then he came out and stood there inside the drug store. I was across the street. In about ten minutes, who came along but Jerry Kameto—Jerry the Pole. Jerry went into the drug store and walked up to the professor. Then they came out and walked down the street together, me after them. They got into a cab and drove over to N Street. They went into a house there and they didn't come out.

"Well, after about half an hour I asked a kid if he knew who lived in the house and the kid said no one, so I went up to the door and rang the bell and nobody answered. So I tried the door and went in. The kid was right. There wasn't anybody there. And the only thing I could figure was that the professor and the Pole went out the back door and gave me the slip."

"Did they know you were tagging them?" Packer asked. "Is that why they went into the house and out the back door?"

"Well, I don't know, captain. They didn't act as if they knew. You can usually tell when a guy knows he's being tailed. The professor didn't wiggle a hair. He didn't know I was there. I'm pretty sure of that. It's my idea they went in there to meet someone and went out the back door with him. I'm pretty sure that's what happened, because some kids playing out back said they saw three men coming towards them from that house."

"And what did you do then?"

"Well, I looked around but I couldn't pick them up. They must have gone out to the next street and caught a cab—or got into their own car—or something. I couldn't help losing them, captain."

"All right," Packer said. "Maybe it wasn't so dumb. The thing for you to do now is to get over to Davis's house right away and wait for him to show up. When he does, pick him up and bring him in. I've got a warrant for his arrest and the charge is murder."

Maguire whistled. "So he's the guy, hey?"

"He's the guy you're to bring in. Don't lose him this time."

"I won't," Maguire promised, and went out. The telephone rang. Bloomingdale answered and listened intently.

"Good!" he exclaimed. "Good! Get the doctor working on him. Let me know when they've got him so he knows what he's talking about." He hung up and faced Packer. "The bullet they dug out of Crane was fired from Harry Tark's gun. We're getting somewhere, captain. When we get a statement out of Tark, we'll get even further."

"*If* you get a statement out of him," Packer said. "No one's been able to get a statement out of that hophead yet. He just doesn't know the answers."

"He'll know 'em this time. This time we've got him where we want him. We've never had him dead to rights before."

The captain nodded and fell silent. After a few minutes he looked up and asked: "What's Professor Bailey saying, if anything?"

"Not a thing," Bloomingdale replied. "I came back from there two minutes before you came in. He lies in his bed looking pretty ghastly and denying he killed Yerkes or that he knows anything about it. Even denies he was here. He just sticks to his first story about going for a walk with Davis. I didn't press him much. There'll be plenty of time for that when he gets on his feet."

He reached then for the telephone. "Get me police headquarters," he said. And waiting, informed Packer: "I'm going to have Jerry the Pole picked up. You might interview him at headquarters."

"Good," the captain agreed. "Ask them to send word here when they find him."

# 17

# THURSDAY 3 P.M.

Patrolman Kurtz, on duty outside the bedroom of Professor Hardwick Bailey, dozed in his chair and dreamed pleasant dreams. Blissfully he dreamed of family and hopes. . . . His daughter, Josephine, who could dance on her toes and who danced on the stage in New York, with a group of a dozen or more girls who all danced the same steps at once and made a very pretty picture in fluffy white gowns and halos. Patrolman Kurtz dreamed now of his Josephine as the reigning belle of them all. He could see all of New York bowing down to her, and bowing down very nicely. Then all of Europe bowed down to her. Even the crowned heads bowed down to her. She had a grand stage name that wasn't exactly Kurtz and wasn't exactly anything else. It was something indefinite but they still (the ones who knew her well) called her Josie, and she was very gracious to them. The sleeping Patrolman Kurtz grinned with much pride.

There was music for Josephine to dance to. There were drums and flutes and all the rest. There was even, faintly, the crisp musical tinkling of breaking glass, representing, maybe, something in the dance. From far away came that sound of breaking glass, as though from somewhere outside the dream. Officer Kurtz stirred a little, licked his lips, hugged his paunch and dreamed on.

The rest of the dream went on pleasantly. There were no more tinklings of broken glass, but the music with all its drums and whistles and fiddles and harps played on and on, and then a voice began to sing, to sing and soar—to soar, then, alarmingly. It became, suddenly, a desperate kind of singing. It rose and rose, broke away from the music. The music fell all to pieces with a dismal clash and still the voice rose and rose and grew louder and louder. Until all at once it became a hoarse, hysterical shriek.

Officer Kurtz leaped to his feet, out of his dream and back into his life, his blood running cold, the shriek truly ringing in his ears; the heart-sickening shriek of a sick man in fearful terror.

And suddenly all was quiet. And as suddenly, to Officer Kurtz, standing in that queer land between sleep and waking, there came the sound of running footsteps in the corridor below.

The voice of the maid, whose name was Annie, called sharply up the stairs: "Oh, for God's sake! For God's sake, what's the matter?"

Officer Kurtz knew by now where he was; exactly where he was. He whirled about, snatched at the knob of the door to Professor Bailey's room and thrust it open.

The maid came running up the stairs and squirmed past Kurtz. There on the floor, face down, crumpled in a heap, lying as limp and forlorn as a bundle of old clothes, was Professor Bailey.

He lay quite still. His hands were twisted beneath him. He had fallen forward on his face.

The maid screamed. "Oh, God! Professor! They've killed him too! Oh, God!" She ran out of the room, bursting into tears as she went, her sobs loud and frantic.

Gingerly, hesitantly, Officer Kurtz knelt beside the crumpled form and placed an ear below the professor's left shoulder-blade, listening intently for any sign of life, wondering whether to keep hands off, as he must if the man was dead, or to administer first aid if he was yet alive. . . .

Then, as he listened for a heart beat, his glance, wandering across the carpeted floor, was caught by the glint of bright pieces of glass upon the floor.

He jerked away from the body and stared at the window. The left pane was broken. There was a jagged hole the size of a man's fist. . . .

# 18
## THURSDAY 3 P.M.

This theory persisted in Ben Ingram's mind: Yerkes, he argued to himself, wanted to talk with me. He left me a note asking me to come to his office. He had never before left me a note except when he had come to the conclusion of one of his investigations. He said once that he wanted to hash the whole thing over with me first before he went to the police. And once he wanted me to be present when he confronted the wrongdoer with the fact that the truth was out. On those occasions he had asked me to come and see him in his Chatham House office. That second time, he wrote or telephoned to the wrongdoer requesting him to be there at a certain time. Did he do that this time? Did that wrongdoer, that criminal, come by such an invitation and, finding that Yerkes knew too much, kill him to silence him?

Months before, at a time when Yerkes, gaunt and fretting, had gone up to the cemetery on the hill where Oscar Coombs had been laid to rest, Ingram, strolling idly past the burial grounds, had seen Yerkes standing moodily at the foot of Coombs's grave: standing with chin in hand, studying now the earth, now the sky, then moving away at a slow pace between the graves, returning to Coombs's grave again, looking away down the hill at the little realm of the university, a frown of thoughtfulness on his brow; turning at length away and striding to the cemetery gate—where Ingram fell in with him.

Surprised, a little startled at Ingram's presence, Yerkes had looked up quickly.

"Something on your mind, Philip?" Ingram asked.

For a moment or two Yerkes was silent. Then he glanced back into the cemetery. "Coombs and I were good friends," he said. "He was a hard-shelled old man but he had his soft spots, and I think one of them was for me. I can't quite get over his going out the way he did."

"He was despondent," Ingram reminded him. "He had just lost his daughter. She was a fine woman, Philip. It was a great blow to him. He had so few friends. I suppose he thought he had nothing left to live for. They used to say he gave whatever love he was capable of to the daughter—what was her name?—Jacqueline."

Yerkes nodded. They moved away from the cemetery gate. Yerkes's nod at the daughter's name changed automatically to a shaking of the head in a slow negative.

"Despondent or not despondent," he said, "Coombs wasn't the kind of man to resort to suicide as—as an escape. He was no coward. He was a fighter. That kind doesn't go to pieces, snatch a gun and go out that way. His kind steps up and fights until he's finished. No, Ben; I could understand that such a man might be willing to die, say, that his daughter might live; but I can't believe that he would die because life was too hard to face; even if it was too hard because he had lost the one person who really loved him deeply."

"He might have been ill, overwrought."

"He wasn't. And he wasn't as despondent as some people think. As a matter of fact, a very curious determination took hold of him shortly after Jacqueline died. I know. I saw a great deal of him at the time. I thought he needed companionship and made it a point to give him mine. There was something on his mind then; something, I was impressed, that he had been afraid of before, but which now he was determined to face. I don't know if it had anything to do with Jacqueline's death. I didn't talk with him about it. I wanted to, but hesitated. I was with him the night before he died, Ben, and I tell you the man was not despondent."

"See here," Ingram put in then: "are you trying to tell me that he was murdered?"

Yerkes put away the idea with a gesture of the hand. "I'm not trying to tell you anything. I'm absolutely in the dark myself, so I've nothing to tell."

"Police experts said it was suicide beyond any shadow of doubt," Ingram insisted.

"I know. And very likely they're right. I don't know why I should feel the way I do. It's probably nothing but imagination."

They had walked on then in silence and when talk came again it was on another subject. . . . And Yerkes had never thereafter spoken to Ingram about his theory of Coombs's death.

But it was too plain to Ingram now that Yerkes had been firmly convinced. It had been no mere passing hunch, forgotten in a day by Yerkes. He had gone ahead, made a positive theory of his hunch, built a case, found the murderer—and had then followed Coombs abruptly in death.

Ben Ingram, walking on the outskirts of the university neighborhood, sought out a certain small, quiet street, went down to its end, mounted the steps of a small white house and stood waiting for an answer to his ring.

After a few minutes the door opened silently and a stout gray-haired woman stood before him, peering at him over spectacles hooked precariously on her ears and set midway down her nose.

"How do you do, Mrs. Garrett?" Ingram began. The woman, stiffening immediately with unmistakable hostility, glared at him.

"I do pretty well. What do you want?"

"Don't you remember me? I'm Professor Ingram. I was a friend of Professor Coombs."

She snapped sharply: "He had no friends. He never had friends."

Ingram said: "Believe me, I was indeed his friend. May I come in and talk with you for a few minutes?"

She hesitated. She had been Coombs's housekeeper. Hers was much the same crisp, antagonistic temperament as her master's had been. She seemed to consider the advisability of admitting even one who protested his friendship so sincerely. Then, surveying Ingram from head to foot, and with a scowl tinged with suspicion, she stepped back.

"Come in."

She turned her back on him and went into a small living room. Hat in hand he followed. She seated herself in a straight-backed chair and motioned him into another.

"Now, what do you want?"

The professor reflected momentarily. Her hostile attitude made it difficult.

"First of all," he began, "I must assure you that I was Professor Coombs's friend. I know that friendship wasn't exactly lavished on him and that he was a lonely man. But I want you to know that I always liked and respected him, and because of that I ask you to listen to what I have to say and give me what help you can."

"I'm listening."

"I suppose," he said, "that you've read in the papers about the death of Professor Yerkes and of a student named Crane?"

Mrs. Garrett sat back and placed her hands firmly on the arms of the chair. "I have."

"Well, Mrs. Garrett," Ingram pursued, "to be as brief as possible, there's a killer loose and in our very midst. He murdered Professor Yerkes, I am convinced, because of something Yerkes knew; and I hold to the belief that the dangerous information concerned the death of Professor Coombs. I mean, in short, that Yerkes had discovered that Professor Coombs had not died by suicide but had been murdered, and that this discovery brought Yerkes's own death yesterday in his office."

Ingram paused. The lips of the woman had become taut and pallid and the knuckles that gripped the chair stood out white and hard.

"I've come to ask you, therefore, to tell me if you can give me any clue, any hint whatsoever, concerning any person—man or woman—with whom Professor Coombs had had any dealing that might have led to his murder. Can you think of anyone? Can you give me the name or even the description of any such person?"

He paused again now. Mrs. Garrett's lips remained hard, her glance was still fixed on him, but her hands loosened their grip on the arms of the chair and folded themselves firmly in her lap.

"You're talking nonsense," she declared. "Everybody knows Professor Coombs killed himself. This talk of murder is foolishness. I ought to know. I found his body, didn't I? There he lay with the gun still in his hand. Why do you talk of murder?"

But her fingers fumbled nervously now, and Ingram, watching her with steady eye, was sure that she was not speaking the whole truth. He knew that she had displayed no emotion during her questioning by the police at the time of Coombs's death. The police, however, had not asked her if she thought her master had been murdered.

"Tell me a little more about it," he urged. "Tell me more of the details."

She said uncomfortably: "I told the police all there was to tell, more than a year ago. Why do you have to dig it all up again?" She sat suddenly and vigorously erect. "Are you trying to say that I killed him?" she demanded. "Is that what you're trying to say?"

"No," he answered. "I'm not trying to say that at all."

"Then why do you want me to give you details? You can read the details in the newspapers. They had every word I said, didn't they? Go get the old newspapers and read it there."

He persisted patiently: "But, you see, I'm looking at it from a different angle now, and anything that you could think of that might be compatible with a theory of murder—"

"I don't know any more than I told then," she broke in sharply. "I was in bed. I heard a shot. I came downstairs and found him in the study. I telephoned the police. And that's all. There's nothing more to tell!"

He eyed her almost with suspicion now, for the force of a powerful inner confusion had flung itself into her limbs. Her voice trembled and rose to a higher pitch as she finished her explanation. She began to shake violently. And he said to her:

"I could be more certain that there's nothing more to tell, Mrs. Garrett, if you didn't tremble so."

She was gray-faced now and she got to her feet with a sudden command of the situation.

"I'll ask you to leave, professor!" she cried. "I don't like this questioning. You aren't the police and I don't have to answer. And there isn't anything to answer anyway! I'm an old woman and you've come here to bully and threaten me—and I won't stand for any more of it!"

She stood facing him dramatically. He rose, shrugged uncomfortably. "I'm sorry," he said. "Good day, Mrs. Garrett."

And he went out of the house and turned his steps back to the university campus.

# 19
## THURSDAY 3:15 P.M.

The outer door of Chatham House rattled violently, and the knob twisted as if in the hand of one in great stress.

Patrolman Anderson, on duty at the door, opened it and faced the thin, dark young man who stood there.

"What do you want?" he asked. "Who are you?"

"I want to see the district attorney. My name's Luciano. I want to see Mr. Bloomingdale or Captain Packer—whoever's here. It's very urgent."

Captain Packer, coming to the door of Ingram's office, called out to Anderson: "Let him in. Come in, Luciano."

Luciano strode nervously across the vestibule and down the corridor. He wore no hat. His hair was slightly disheveled and there was a frightened look in his eyes.

"What does he want?" Bloomingdale asked, looking up from a police report on the desk before him.

Luciano stood in the office doorway, wringing his hands. Gone entirely was the smooth, easy-going manner he had worn before.

"What is it?" the captain asked.

"I've been shot at!" Luciano said, swallowing hard. "They tried to kill me! in my own room. The shot missed me, I think, by inches. For God's sake, captain, what is this—a massacre?"

The captain stood aside. "Come in. Sit down there. Now tell us what happened."

"I told you what happened!" Luciano said irritably. "I was sitting at my desk. My room's on the ground floor at the back of

Rochester Hall. The window was open and my back was to it. I was trying to study and all of a sudden there was an explosion behind me and something struck the wall in front of me. I dropped down to the floor and waited. Nothing more happened. I waited a few minutes. Then I got up. I went and looked out the window. There wasn't any one there. Then two of the boys from down the hall came in. They asked if I'd heard a shot. Then we looked at the wall and there was a bullet hole there. For God's sake, Mr. Bloomingdale, isn't anyone safe around here?"

Bloomingdale bit his lip and studied Luciano's frightened face.

"You'd better go over, captain," he said, "and have a look."

"Right," said the captain. "Come along, Luciano. We'll go and see what there is to see."

He picked up his hat and motioned Luciano ahead of him. Still with much agitation, Luciano went out.

Bloomingdale leaned back in his chair, scowling out into the corridor. Then he picked up the police report on yesterday's happenings at Chatham House and the police draughtman's chart of the building and the surrounding grounds.

He had no sooner done so than the telephone rang with a sharpness that made him wince. He tossed the papers on to the desk and picked up the receiver.

"Hello. Bloomingdale speaking."

"Hello. This is Officer Kurtz, on duty at this Professor Bailey's house. Something happened here, Mr. Bloomingdale. I think someone ought to come over right away. This professor passed out cold on the floor in his room and—"

"What! Passed out cold! Is he dead?"

"No," Kurtz replied. "But I guess he's the next thing to it. . . ."

# 20
## THURSDAY 3:20 P.M.

The captain motioned Luciano into the back of the police car and himself got in beside the patrolman at the wheel.

"How do we get to your dormitory?" he asked.

The car was headed north. "You can drive straight up here," Luciano directed. "Turn left at North Park and then it's at the other side of the campus."

"Let's go," the captain said. They shot swiftly to North Park; turned west and sped toward the dormitory section of the university.

They passed group after group of the red brick colonial style buildings, until Luciano said: "The next one," and the car came to a stop at the main entrance and Luciano and the captain stepped out.

"It's this way," Luciano said. They went into the building, walked down a corridor to the rear, then turned right and went down another corridor. Luciano, halting before a door marked 14, thrust his key in the lock.

"In here," he said, opened the door and moved aside to let the captain enter.

Packer stood outside for perhaps half a minute, looking into the room, his gaze traveling from corner to corner of the place. This room was the study. The door to the bedroom was at the left. A desk stood in the middle of the study, a swivel chair before it, its back to the two windows. Both windows were shut and, the captain could see, locked.

The captain entered now. Luciano, following, closed the door.

"Now," the captain directed, "show me where you were sitting."

Luciano seated himself in the swivel chair. Texts and notebooks were open on the desk before him. "I was sitting like this," he explained, "and studying. That window—" he paused, swung about in the chair and pointed to the window at his right "—was open. The other one was closed. I didn't hear any sound—any sound of anyone coming up to the window. I had no warning at all. There was the *bang* of the shot and the noise of something hitting the wall, and then I ducked."

"I see," said the captain. His eyes went from the window to Luciano and thence to the wall beyond. He went to that wall and examined a bullet hole there. With a pocket knife he dug out the bullet, examined it briefly, then dropped it into his pocket.

Next, standing with his back to the bullet hole, he looked along the line in which the bullet had sped. "Sit exactly as you were sitting—or as near as you can," he requested and, as Luciano bent forward a little over his books, continued grimly: "I should say, Luciano, that you're alive by a bare matter of inches. I think that if you had been sitting erect in that chair and a little further to your right, you'd have been killed."

Luciano was pale. The captain went on: "When the shot came, you say you dropped down. Just how?"

Luciano pushed back the chair and dropped down between chair and desk. Then he got up.

"How long did you stay down there?"

"I don't know exactly. A minute—probably more."

"Did you look back at the window to see who was there?"

"Not until I got up."

"Show me how you got up."

Luciano said, without demonstrating: "Well, I crawled along the floor there, close to the desk, and got behind it. I looked around the side of it, saw no one, and then I went to the window and looked out."

The captain went to the window indicated. "You closed and locked this after looking out?"

"Yes. Then the boys came in and we found the bullet hole. We opened the window again, looked out once more, then we closed and locked it."

The captain threw the latch open, pushed the window up and thrust out his head. A mere five feet below the window sill was the ground, or rather a brick walk, beyond which was a border of bushes. The walk extended along the rear of the building, running in both directions.

The captain now examined the outer sill. The dark-gray dust that lay there had been disturbed, wiped away in a single spot at the edge of the sill.

Luciano, standing at the captain's side, pointed to that spot. "There!" he declared; "there's where he reached up and put his hand to take aim."

The captain bent closer to the spot. Then, straightening up, he looked over his shoulder at the bullet hole in the wall.

"I'd like to use your phone, please," he said.

Luciano indicated the instrument on the desk. The captain sat down and called headquarters. "Hello. Give me Jacobs. . . . Hello, Jacobs? Captain Packer. Send me a fingerprint man, will you? Yes, right away. Over to the university. Rochester Hall. Room Number 14. I'll be waiting."

He hung up and pushed away the telephone. Abruptly now he swung about in the swivel chair to face Luciano who stood beside the desk.

"Well, Mr. Luciano," he said, "and why did they shoot at you?"

Luciano frowned and he considered the matter a moment.

"I don't know. I hadn't thought about it. My mind's been taken up entirely with the single fact that they did shoot."

"I can understand that," the captain told him, "but there must have been a reason, of course. You see, you're in a rather unique position. Two men have been killed and your life has been attempted. You're the only one of three marked men who can talk. I'm inclined to think that if Professor Yerkes and Leonard Crane could talk, they could say why they were killed. Now, can you tell me why anyone should want to kill you? Is there anything you know that would be dangerous to the killer of these other two men? Is there anything you know or anything you've done that would make anyone want to put you out of the way?"

For a moment Luciano seemed a little bewildered. He passed a hand over his brow and sat down in an armchair.

"I don't know," he said. "I can't think of anything—nor of anyone." He paused, plucking thoughtfully at his lip. "Probably the killer knows that I heard the voices in Yerkes's office just before he died."

"But you didn't recognize the other voices besides Yerkes's, did you?"

"No, but the killer may not know that. He's probably taking no chances."

"Hm. . . . You told your story about hearing voices upstairs to how many people?"

"I told it to President Meade, Dr. Royal and Professor Ingram."

"All right. And then you told it to Mr. Bloomingdale and to me. Now, there's no one else in the world can know that story, is there?"

"No."

"Then there's no one else in the world knows you heard those voices. Assuming, now, that neither I nor Mr. Bloomingdale fired the shot at you—and it's a fair thing to assume—which of those three other men, would you say, was afraid you might recognize them as the speakers and sneak around back here and take a pot shot at you? Which ones?"

Luciano's puzzlement deepened the furrows in his brow.

"Well," he reasoned, "it couldn't have been Professor Ingram. I met him in East Park when I left Chatham House."

"Yes. And Ingram, within a matter of a few minutes thereafter, located both President Meade and Dr. Royal at their offices by telephoning to report the crime. No, Luciano, we can't incriminate any of those gentlemen.

"Now, stop and think. Would there be anything else that anyone would want to shoot you for? Do you know anything else connected with this matter—something that's, say, slipped your mind, or that you don't think is important? Believe me, it's all

important; every bit of it; and what looks like the least significant fact may turn out to be the best clue. Come now, think.
What do you say?"

Reflecting again, Luciano declared: "There's not a thing. I
can't think of a thing I haven't told. There's nothing I'm hiding
voluntarily. There's no one I know about who'd want to do me
harm."

The captain rubbed his jaw. "And yet someone does want
to do you harm. . . . Well, you keep turning these things over
in your mind, young man, and if you think of anything you've
forgotten at the moment, get in touch with me at once. It may
mean your life. . . ."

# 21
## THURSDAY 3:30 P.M.

Annie, the maid, opened to Bloomingdale's ring.

Bloomingdale strode in. "Where's Professor Bailey?"

The maid gulped. "Upstairs. In his room with that policeman."

Motioning brusquely to the two plainclothes men who accompanied him, Bloomingdale made quickly for the stairway. At the head of the stairs Mary Bailey met them. Whitefaced, she spoke:

"Father's in there."

Swiftly Bloomingdale moved past her, entered the open doorway of the bedroom.

Patrolman Kurtz sat in a chair beside the bed. Professor Bailey, his face a ghastly white, lay limp and flat on his back. Kurtz had a bottle of smelling salts in his hand. He got up as Bloomingdale came in.

"He isn't dead," he said in response to Bloomingdale's glance. "I brought him around with this." He held up the bottle of salts.

Bloomingdale took it out of his hand and sat down in the chair. Leaning toward the professor, he said:

"Bailey. Professor Bailey. Can you hear me? This is Bloomingdale, the district attorney. Open your eyes, if you can."

Mary Bailey stood behind them, wringing her hands.

"Father," she called softly.

Professor Bailey opened his eyes and his dull gaze went to Bloomingdale's face and then to his daughter's. "Mary," he said, and raised a weak hand.

Mary pushed past the men and sat down on the bed, took her father's hand. "Father, darling, would you rather not speak with these men now?"

"I'll speak with them," Bailey replied. "Now's as good a time as any. But will you—will you, dear, please go out of the room?"

"Of course, darling." She got up and said to Bloomingdale: "The doctor will be here any minute. Please don't upset him any more than you can help."

"All right, Miss Bailey."

She went out, closed the door. Bloomingdale looked up at Officer Kurtz. "Tell me what happened."

"Well, it was like this," Kurtz began. "I was outside the door when there came the sound of glass broken and then the professor hollered. I came running in and found him on the floor. The window was broken and he lay all of a heap. He was unconscious. I couldn't seem to hear hardly any heart beat at all. He was lying there on his face. I left him there and went downstairs and called you.

"Well, I had a little trouble getting the line and I was gone, say, a little more than five minutes. When I came back, he was up on his feet and over there in front of the fireplace, holding on to the mantelpiece. And the funny thing of it was, Mr. Bloomingdale, he'd been burning something there and he had the poker in his hand and he was crushing the ashes into powder. There was the smell of burned paper in here.

"When I came in he sort of hung on to the mantelpiece a little and then keeled over and I caught him and put him on the bed. The maid was downstairs having hysterics. About two minutes later the daughter came in. She'd gone out on an errand about half an hour before. She got those salts and we brought him around and—well, that's all."

Bloomingdale got up and went over to the window. He picked up several of the pieces of broken glass that lay on the floor. He looked out the window, down upon a flourishing English garden through which ran walks made of wide slabs of slate. One of these walks lay directly below the window that had been broken and ran back to a gate in the fence at the rear. Beyond the fence was a narrow, private way, the other side of which was bordered thickly with maples.

From the window Bloomingdale went to the fireplace and, stooping before the hearth, examined the little heap of ashes on the bottom of the otherwise clean stone. The ashes, as Kurtz had said, had been ground into fine powder. From a corner of the fireplace Bloomingdale picked up a smooth stone a little smaller than his fist.

He stood up now, weighing the stone in his fingers. He turned back to the bed. Professor Bailey's eyes followed his every move. Bloomingdale reseated himself in the bedside chair.

"Well, professor, suppose you tell us what all the excitement's about. What came through the window?" He held up the stone. "Someone sent you a message wrapped around this, didn't they? Don't you think you ought to tell us what it was—and who sent it?"

The professor closed his eyes wearily. "It isn't necessary," he said, "to go into that. I'm fed up with this whole thing, Mr. Bloomingdale. I know there's no use dodging you nor lying to you any longer. I killed Philip Yerkes. And I arranged to have the student, Crane, put out of the way, as well. You'd better take me away to your jail."

Bloomingdale, who had been pretty sure of Bailey, had not, however, been prepared for a swift, quiet confession. For several seconds he was dumb. Officer Kurtz stared almost in horror at the worn, tired face on the pillow. The two plainclothes men exchanged glances of surprise.

Bloomingdale prompted: "Tell us about it. Tell us what happened."

Still with his eyes closed, Bailey continued: "It's quite simple. I shan't tell you why I killed him. That would be unnecessarily disagreeable. But I had a very good reason. I went to Chatham House, talked with Yerkes for a while and then shot him. Then, when I had done this thing, I came out of his office and met Professor Davis, who had come out of his own office at the sound of the shot. I told him what I had done. Charitably enough—he has always been a good friend—he offered to see that I got away quickly. He suggested the rear door. We went out together, through the brush behind Chatham House, and away from there."

He paused.

"What did you do with the gun?" Bloomingdale asked grimly.

"Disposed of it," Bailey said. "I gave it to someone."

"To whom?"

"To the same person whom I paid to hire a professional killer to put Crane out of the way."

"And why did you want Crane out of the way?"

"Because he knew that it was I who had killed Yerkes. He was in the building at the time."

"And what is the name of the person who hired the professional killer for you?"

"I shan't tell that. I shall not incriminate any one else. That's all I have to say. Do you want me to come with you now?"

"Do you think you can manage it?"

"Yes. I've been pretending much of my weakness. I'm strong enough to go."

He opened his eyes, threw aside the bedclothes, got weakly to his feet. "If you'll let me get dressed—"

Bloomingdale rose. Soberly he said: "Officer Kurtz will stay with you while you dress."

He went to the door. The two plainclothes men went out with him.

## 22
## THURSDAY 4:00 P.M.

From Mrs. Garrett's Ingram trudged back unhappily to his home. He was in a dull confusion of thought. He was no detective, no lawyer. He did not know how to handle these things. He felt, now, the handicap of his semi-cloistered life. He envied the swift-thinking, swift-moving Bloomingdale; the practical, hard-as-rock Packer. Book knowledge he had far more than they; but they had a knowledge of life and men that one does not learn from books. He would go blundering where his nose led him in this case; while these men, these manhunters, their senses whetted to this kind of chase, would go in a business-like way into the task of sorting out facts and people, and then swiftly penetrate into the heart of the mystery. Packer and Bloomingdale were known to be such a pair. Together they had made a remarkable record. The newspapers had said so.

And yet Ingram felt that he must, in his little, futile way, plod on and ever on until there was nowhere left to go. He must leave no stone unturned; no stone, however insignificant to the police, must lie and hide any secret. He would not believe, could not believe that his dearest friends had killed his other good friend. Or if they had, there must be a reason that somehow would make their crime look less black than it seemed.

Why, he *knew* these men; knew their innermost hearts; had known them since he had known anyone, in his cradle. They were the kindest, most gentle of men. Thaddeus Davis who, though he had made him skilful in boxing and wrestling when he was yet very young, had always told him never to use his skill nor his strength unless there was a sure need. Tall Tad Davis, who had taken him to the zoo one day and showed him first a jolly good-natured old bear that romped with the children and hurt no one, and showed him next a deadly rattlesnake that struck savagely at a stick thrust between its screening.

"It is good," Tad had said, "to be like both of these creatures. You will some day grow up to be, in your way, as strong as a bear. You will be skilful in the arts of fighting (when I get through with you, young man). Learn from this bear to be friendly and good-natured and to inflict your strength and your claws on no one who lets you alone. Learn even to be tolerant with those who do not let you alone but who are no match for you. Push them away but do not strike. But when you find those who would do you harm and can do you harm, then strike; strike as fast as that snake and with the same deadliness and accuracy."

Reflecting soberly on these old memories, Ingram worried painfully concerning what might have happened to cause Tad Davis to act toward Yerkes, according to his precept of the zoo. Had Yerkes meant him harm? Had Yerkes somehow intended harm to Davis and Bailey both? And had they struck him down before he could do that harm? Had Yerkes, in some incomprehensible way, been a secret blackguard?

Had—and the thought came with a scorching pain—had Davis and Bailey been involved in the death of Coombs? Had they struck at Yerkes, and again at Crane, to keep their first crime a secret?

He began to worry now about Mary Bailey. He had not seen her since her father's arrest this morning. He had telephoned the house as soon as he had learned that Bailey and Davis were to be arrested, but Mary had gone early to Dr. Royal's house to ask some questions concerning her father's condition, and he had not reached her.

And he felt guilty now that he had not gone to the Davis home to stand by Mrs. Davis when the shock of her husband's arrest came to her. And so, on reaching his home, he went to the telephone, and even as he laid a hand upon it, it rang and he answered in a preoccupied manner.

It was Mary. Her voice, alarmed, whipped him from preoccupation to an acute intentness.

"Yes, Mary, what is it?"

There was a sob in her voice. "Ben!" she cried. "They've taken Father away! This morning they placed him under arrest, left an officer here and allowed him to stay. But now he's confessed! Confessed, Ben! To those awful murders! Oh, Ben, I don't know what to do I'm frantic and half insane! They've taken him away—taken him to jail; and they say they'll hold him there without bail until his trial. Oh, Ben, what does it all mean?"

Ingram caught his breath and gripped the telephone so fiercely that an aching came into his wrists.

"Mary, hold on!" he urged. "I'll come over. I'll come over and talk with you. Please don't go to pieces. I'll drive over at once."

He hung up and turned away from the instrument, then remembering that he must call Mrs. Davis, went back to do so. Mrs. Davis herself answered. Her voice was bright and untouched by emotion.

"No, Ben," she said, "Tad isn't here. He went out very early this morning, on business. I did expect him for lunch, but he phoned and said that he wouldn't be able to get here and didn't know exactly when he would be back. That nice police captain has been looking for him too, but I wasn't able to tell him, either, where Tad is. Shall I have him phone you when he comes in?"

A cold sweat broke out on Ingram's brow. The captain had gone over to put Davis under arrest and, not finding him there, had left undivulged the reason for his visit.

And of course the papers, though they might already have the story of Bailey's arrest, would not yet mention Davis. It was likely that she did not know even of Bailey's arrest, for, in all probability, she would not see a paper containing that news until the evening delivery. Her mind was yet free of the frightful worries that would soon enough be hers.

"Don't bother to have him phone," Ingram told her. "I'll get in touch with him sometime during the evening. How are you, dear?" he asked.

"Very well. I've been upset, of course, by the dreadful death of Philip Yerkes. And that poor young student. But I don't know much about it. Tad has absolutely refused to let me read the newspaper accounts. He said it would only upset me. Why, believe it or not, he's actually stopped the paper delivery here. I haven't the faintest idea of what's going on in the world. He's even forbidden me to listen to the news on the radio."

Ingram mopped his brow. "Tad's quite right, dear. The details are pretty harrowing, and it wouldn't do you any good to wallow through them."

"I know. I don't mind. Tad'll tell me what there is to tell when he comes in. I can't imagine where he's gone, though. It must be very important."

"No doubt."

"When," she asked, "are you coming over to see us—you and Mary?"

"Oh, soon. I've been terribly busy—but almost any day now."

He went quickly out of the house then and to the garage and drove out his car. Heading north, he swung into Aldrich Road and then into Price Street.

Mary answered the bell. She was white and frightened and her eyes were moist with restrained tears, tears that broke furiously when she saw Ben Ingram. He took her in his arms to give her what little comfort he might.

"Darling," he said, "it can't be as bad as it looks. Things never are. There must be some explanation—something we don't know about—something we'll learn if we keep our heads. Don't cry so, Mary darling."

"But what explanation can there be?" she sobbed. "What other explanation? What more do we have to know? He's confessed, Ben. Confessed! Oh, it's the end of everything. Poor dear Father! I never thought that he would hurt a fly—and now, this! It's too terrible, Ben!"

"I know," he said gently. "I know. Mary, I'll go down to the jail and talk with him. I tell you there must be more to it than we know."

"Oh, what can there be; and why should he hide anything anyhow? Why should he confess if it weren't true?"

"I don't know," he told her frankly. "I don't know what it's all about, except that Davis is involved too, and no one seems to have found out how, just yet. And so far as I know, Tad hasn't been arrested yet. It would almost seem, Mary, that he's disappeared. He hasn't been home all day, and I know that the police are looking for him with a warrant."

"It'll kill Mrs. Davis," Mary said, "when they arrest him."

"I'm afraid of that," Ingram agreed. "I'm afraid of what it'll do to her heart. It's none too strong. She'll need help, Mary. We'll have to stand by her when she needs us. You'll have to pull yourself together, dear, and help."

Mary stopped weeping, dried her eyes. "I'll be all right. I won't let go again. I'll stand by her when the time comes. I'll do my best."

With furrowed brow Ingram regarded her. "Tell me, dear; they didn't take your father out of his sick bed, did they? He was in no condition to go out. I thought they were going to keep him in custody here and—"

"He insisted," she explained. "He insisted that he was well enough to go. He seemed almost anxious. I don't know why. But it had something to do with what was thrown through the window and—"

"What was thrown through the window?" Ingram asked quickly. "What window? What happened, Mary?"

"Why, someone threw a stone with some kind of message wrapped around it; threw it into his bedroom—broke the window. It was just after that that he went into a terrible kind of hysteria and told them then that he was the—" she shuddered "—the murderer."

"Do they know what the message was; who it was from?"

"No. He burned it in the fireplace and he won't tell what it was. But whatever it was, it was the immediate cause—I'm sure—of his confession."

Ingram got up and paced the floor, his agitation growing.

"If that message precipitated his confession," he said, "we've got to find out who sent it and what was in it. A clue lies there—and we must find out what it is. I tell you, Mary, somehow—somehow we haven't got the truth—not the whole truth."

"But he won't talk about it, Ben. He won't listen to any questions about it. He says that he's confessed and that's all that's important. Do you think, Ben, do you really think, that he's not telling the truth—that he's shielding someone—that he's shielding—"

She paused and met his eyes, which were grave and filled with pain.

"Tad Davis?" he finished her query. "I don't know. Maybe. Maybe it's someone else. Or something else altogether. Something we can't see, from where we are. Mary, your father's got to talk. I'm going down to the jail and make him talk!"

Mary said: "You can't bully him into talking, Ben. You can't force anything out of Father."

"I won't bully him," Ingram promised. He took his hat from the chair where he had tossed it. "I'm just going to ask him to listen to reason."

# 23
## THURSDAY 5:00 P.M.

Captain Packer came back to Chatham House from Luciano's dormitory and found Johnny Mortimer, the assistant district attorney, in Ingram's office, looking out the window into the thicket behind the building.

"Hello," Packer greeted. "Where's Bloomingdale?"

Johnny Mortimer turned. "Gone back to the courthouse with Bailey. Say, you don't know, do you? Bailey up and confessed."

Packer's eyes widened. "Confessed? To what? When?"

"Just now, it seems. Owned up to murdering Yerkes and hiring a gunman to do away with young Crane. Nice old gentleman, don't you think?"

Packer whistled softly. "What prompted this all of a sudden?"

Mortimer shrugged. "Don't know. I just came back from Corvetti's. Bloomingdale stopped in here for a few minutes to leave word to tell you what had happened. I didn't even get a chance to tell him about Corvetti. He said you were over at this—what's his name?—Luciano's place, looking at a bullet hole. What happened over there?"

The captain sat down. "Tell me," he pressed, "did Bailey involve Davis?"

"I think not. He involved nobody but himself."

"Is he telling the truth?"

"So far as I know. What about the bullet hole?"

The captain frowned. "More deep stuff. Someone came up to his window with a gun, took a shot at him and beat it. I had

145

Munyon down looking for fingerprints on the window sill. He says there's nothing but smudges—no good at all."

"Does Luciano know why he was fired at? Does he know something they want to put him out of the way for?"

"He says no. He can't give any reason for the attempt."

"Well, what do you think they shot at him for?" Mortimer asked. "Pure pleasure?"

"Can't say. I quizzed him. He says he hasn't any enemies—not the kind that would want to do him off."

"Of course there's this angle," Mortimer offered. "Say, they aren't sure whether he knows something or not. They do know he's been quizzed here, same as Crane, and they're taking no chances. If Bailey hired a gunman to put Crane out, he probably wouldn't spare the expense to have the same thing done to Luciano."

In silence Packer fingered the brim of his felt hat, finally putting the hat back on his head.

"Well," he said, "we'll just have to annoy Bailey a little on that angle. By the way, what reason did he give for his bloody holiday?"

"None, I believe. Wouldn't give reasons."

The captain cried sharply: "Rot! That isn't a confession. It's a coverup of some kind. You can't tell me! I'm going down there and have a little chat with the gentleman myself."

"I don't know," Mortimer said. "I'm inclined to think the confession's okay, as far as it goes. He isn't telling any more than he has to because he's covering someone else—his friend Davis, who was here with him. That's what I think. Haven't found Davis yet, have you?"

"It looks as if he's given us the slip," the captain said disgustedly. "Say, what are these college professors anyway? Homicidal maniacs? They're clever, I'll say. That's what an education does for you, Mortimer."

Mortimer sniffed. "Doesn't strike me Bailey's been so clever, for all his tremendous education. And Davis will turn up too, sooner or later. When are you going to send out a description?"

"Oh, I don't know. Give him a chance to turn up at home during the day or the evening. If he doesn't come home tonight, then we'll be sure he's playing hookey and we'll broadcast for him."

Mortimer laughed mirthlessly. "Once he sees headlines about Bailey's arrest and confession, you can kiss him good-by. Be sure of that."

Packer showed his hands in a gesture of futility, then changed the subject. "What did Corvetti have to say?"

"Corvetti? Oh, not much. Gave me a good cigar, a long high-ball and a nice fat armchair to park in and said he'd answer all questions including any about his love life."

"I know. That's his old line. But what did he say about Tark?"

"Well, he said that of course Tark had been one of his errand boys during prohibition—used to drive a truck and such—but he says the stories about Tark's being a killer are all wrong. And he said that he doesn't believe Tark had anything to do with the Crane killing, and if he did he was certainly working freelance."

The captain snorted. "Huh! And I suppose he said Tark isn't a hophead and that he doesn't sell Tark the white powder or give it to him when he wants to prime him for a job. No, of course not. There was no use talking with him. We've been trying to get something on Corvetti since—since before you were even in law school, Mortimer; but he's always innocent as a two-year-old. Well, it doesn't matter. We've got Tark and we've got Bailey. And we'll get Davis too—all in good time."

# 24
## THURSDAY 5:57 P.M.

Ingram drove his car into the parking space behind the court-house, went in and inquired the way to Bloomingdale's office. At the end of a long corridor he found the door marked District Attorney. It stood ajar. He knocked and Bloomingdale's voice said: "Come."

Ingram stepped in. Bloomingdale was at his desk. A stenographer, pencil poised over notebook, glanced up.

"Hullo, professor," Bloomingdale greeted. "Something I can do for you?"

"I'd like to ask a favor," Ingram said. "I'd like to have a few words with Professor Bailey."

"About what?" Bloomingdale asked, surprised.

"About this confession. I can't believe, Mr. Bloomingdale, that— You see, I want to talk to him and try to get at the bottom of this thing."

"I was of the opinion," Bloomingdale informed him, "that we had already got to the bottom of it. He signed a confession right here in this office."

"But I'm convinced," Ingram pleaded, "that he's covering up someone; that he confessed in order to—"

"Of course he's covering up someone," Bloomingdale asserted. "We know that. He's covering up Davis, but he isn't doing a very good job. But that doesn't say he wasn't involved himself. I tell you, Ingram, both of those men visited Yerkes. I don't know which of them carried the gun and pulled the trigger, but they were both there, and they left together. We have that from Schultz.

We know that, Ingram. You can't ask me to believe that two and two make anything but four."

Ingram gestured helplessly. "Nevertheless, I'd like to talk with him, if you'll permit it. It can't do any harm—come along if you like—and it may do some good. He's known me ever since I was a child and—"

"But what do you expect to get out of him? Something about Davis? You don't think he'd tell you that, do you?"

"No, I don't mean Davis exactly. Bloomingdale, I don't know what I mean. I simply feel certain that there's a confusion in this thing and I want to talk with him and get it straightened out. Besides, the man needs a friend; needs to know he has someone who'll stand by. His daughter asked me to come. Will you let me see him?"

Bloomingdale moved his shoulders. "Oh, I suppose so. You can see him in his cell." He pressed a button under the edge of his desk.

"Thanks," Ingram said.

A burley, hatless officer came in.

"Take this gentleman," Bloomingdale directed, "across the way. He wants to see Professor Bailey. I'll telephone over."

"Yes, sir," said the officer. "This way."

Ingram followed him down the corridor, down a flight of stairs and through a half-dark passage, then up another flight of stairs at the head of which they were met by another officer.

The first guide turned back. Ingram went on with the second. They went along a stone floor and into a corridor of cells. The officer opened the door of the first cell.

"In here," he said.

Ingram went in. Bailey lay on a narrow cot, eyes closed, his face drawn, lined, death-like. Ingram said softly: "Uncle Hardy."

Bailey opened his eyes. The guard closed the barred door and stood with his back to it. Bloomingdale's orders, of course. He would be able to hear every word.

Bailey licked dry lips. "Ben. What are you doing here?"

Ingram sat down on the edge of the cot. "Standing by, Uncle Hardy. I've come for Mary and myself, to tell you that we want you to let us help you all we can."

Bailey's eyes went from Ingram to the ceiling of his narrow quarters. "I'm afraid it's too late to help me. It's really no use. I've confessed. I've told them the whole story."

"Tell it to me," Ingram urged soberly.

Bailey's eyes were still on the ceiling. "I don't see what good it can do."

"I want to hear it first-hand. The newspapers will distort it. I want to get it straight."

Bailey licked his lips again. "There's nothing to distort," he declared. "I went there and killed him. That's all."

"Why did you kill him?"

"I'm not going to tell that. Don't ask me again. I've told the police I'm not going to tell that."

"Did it have something to do with the death of Oscar Coombs?"

With a strained patience, Bailey protested: "I told you I was not going to talk about it!"

Ingram ventured: "When did you decide to kill him? When did it come into your mind?"

"I don't know," Bailey replied. "I've had it in my mind for some time. I saw it coming. I—I knew that I would have to do it sooner or later."

"And," Ingram went on, "yesterday afternoon you met Tad Davis, went down there with him, went into the building with him and—?"

"That's not true," Bailey cut in. "Davis was in his office at the time. I didn't know he was there. He heard the shot I fired. He came down to Yerkes's office just as I stepped out."

"What did you do then, Uncle Hardy?"

Bailey said wearily: "I didn't know what to do. I told Davis what I had done. He said I had best get out of there right away. He said I had best go by the rear door to avoid meeting anyone coming in at the front. I decided to do that and went downstairs quickly. He came after me. I begged him to let me go alone, but he insisted. We went down into the basement and out into the thicket. We went down the path, out on to the road and then home. . . . Is that all you want to know? Do you have any more questions? Ask them and let me have it over with."

"There is another question. It has to do with conflicting stories. As you know, the student, Luciano, says he went into Chatham House that afternoon and left a theme in your box. We didn't find it there. Did you take it out?"

Bailey nodded. "Yes. I took it out. I stopped in the lower corridor on my way in and opened the box. Force of habit, I suppose. I don't know exactly why I did it."

"You went into Chatham House by which door, the front or the rear?"

"The rear door. I didn't want to be seen."

"I see. Because your purpose in entering was specifically to kill Yerkes. That's so, isn't it?"

"Yes."

"Did you know he was there in his office before you went to Chatham House?"

"Yes. I telephoned him just before I left home."

"He expected you, then?"

"Yes."

"When you spoke with him on the phone, did he ask you to come over, or did you invite yourself?"

"He asked me to come."

"He wanted to discuss something?"

"Yes."

"About Coombs's death?"

"I've told you I won't talk about that."

"Very well. But you knew what he wanted to talk about?"

"Yes."

"And it was that that brought to a head the decision to kill him then?"

"Yes."

"Then I don't believe, Uncle Hardy," Ingram shot out, "that you stopped in the lower hallway to open your theme box—habit or no habit. The will to kill thrusts aside petty habits, Uncle Hardy, and I think—"

Bailey sucked his breath through clenched teeth. His fists were gripped at his sides. He said in a restrained voice:

"It doesn't matter much what you think, Ben. I've told you what happened. That is what happened. If I've established a psychological precedent, write a paper about it. But don't tell me it isn't so. You could write a very pretty paper: Psychological Variations in Murder. You could—"

"Don't," Ingram begged. "Please!"

Bailey lay silent now. After a moment or two Ingram said: "Tad Davis has eluded the police. Did you know that?"

Bailey shook his head. "I didn't know. I don't know why he should run away."

"There's a murder warrant out for him."

"Stupid police! They arrest everybody and anybody. Davis had nothing to do with it."

"But you say that he knew you had killed Yerkes—and he kept that a secret and helped you to get away."

"That is a far cry from murder. He had nothing to do with Yerkes's death. I—and I alone—am guilty."

"Nevertheless, Uncle Tad is missing."

"Panic. That's all. Panic. He'll turn up."

"What makes you so sure?"

"Because he's innocent. They can prove nothing against him."

"They might call him an accessory after the fact."

Bailey said nothing.

"And the fact does remain," Ingram added, "that there is a murder warrant out for him."

"The charge can never be proved."

There was no use arguing further. However, there was no question whatsoever in Ingram's mind now but that Bailey was taking the whole thing upon himself in order to protect someone else, and that someone else must be Thaddeus Davis. Whatever the circumstances were, Bailey felt obligated to assume entire blame. Simple altruism, it might be. (They can put me to death but once, therefore it is best that I take all the blame and let another man have his life.) . . . Or were there other reasons, deeply hidden, even beyond imagination?

He laid a hand on Bailey's arm. Bailey opened his eyes once more. Ingram stood up.

"Uncle Hardy," he said, "Mary and I are with you and will stand by no matter what happens. Never forget that."

Bailey smiled with a faint upturn of the corners of his lips.

"Thank you, Ben. I won't forget. It will make things easier."

Ten minutes later Ingram telephoned to the executor of the Coombs estate, an attorney named Blanding. Blanding, who declared he would be occupied until late in the evening, offered to see Ingram at his, Blanding's, office at ten o'clock that night.

# 25
## THURSDAY 7:05 P.M.

Ingram drove back to the university. He had promised Mary that he would see her as soon as he returned from her father.

She was waiting for him at the door as he came up the steps.

She asked: "Did they—did they let you see him?"

"Yes."

"And how is he? Shouldn't he really be in a hospital instead of in a terrible cell, Ben?"

Ingram entered the house with her. "He seemed to be all right," he told her. "He'll get medical attention there if he needs it. That's scarcely the worst of it."

"What do you mean?"

They went into the living room and sat by the windows.

"He persists," Ingram said, "in his confession. There's no shaking it. I went over it with him. He seemed not unwilling. Perhaps he expected it and wanted to get it over with. But when I tried to point out what I thought were weak spots, things that didn't seem to hold water, he talked me down. He's very eager about this confession, Mary; almost too eager."

"You mean—?"

"I mean that I'm convinced now beyond a doubt that there's more to it than he tells. Whether what he tells is true as far as it goes and there's more to it that he's hiding—or whether it's a story entirely false—that I don't know. But there's something wrong with it, something vitally wrong."

"Is it what you thought before—that he's shielding Tad Davis?"

"I wish I knew. It may be that. It probably is. But I can't get over the uncomfortable, uncanny feeling that there's more to it even than that; more than even shielding Tad Davis. I tell you, Mary, your father was, and still is, in deathly terror of something. Take that message that was thrown through the window. Consider the condition of hysteria into which it threw him. What can it be, Mary? What can it be?"

"I don't know."

Then Ingram asked: "Mary, can you recall just how he acted yesterday, before the murder and after it—anything that he did that seemed strange?"

"No. He was quite cheerful at breakfast, just as usual. I'm sure that if he'd been upset he'd have showed it. He almost always does. He gets quiet or silent when there's something on his mind. He came downstairs looking fresh and rested and he joked a little with me—about you, in fact. He asked me how long it would be before I would be waiting for you to come down to breakfast, and jokingly bemoaned the fact that some day I would desert him for an Ingram."

Ingram took her hand. "Another question. Did he have any visitors—anyone unusual in the past few days; anyone who, in the light of what has happened, might seem to be concerned in this?"

She reflected. Then she said: "No. No strangers have been here. At least, not while I was here. Why—who might have come that you think—?"

"I don't know. I'm just feeling around in the dark." He paused, then went on thoughtfully: "I'd like to check his story. Check it on every angle. I'd like to go upstairs to his study and look through some of his papers. May I? There's a certain paper—and I'd like to see if it's there. You see, he says that he went into Chatham House, opened his theme box and took out a theme by this student, Luciano. I want to see if that paper is there. In the beginning of this thing, there was a conflict between your father's word and Luciano's. Luciano said that he deposited the paper. Your father said first that he hadn't gone to Chatham House, therefore he couldn't have taken out the paper. Now he declares he did take it. I want to check up on that, if possible. Shall we go up and see?"

Mary stood up. "Yes. Let's. What can it mean, though, one way or another?"

Ingram, considering his reply to her question, was some moments in answering. They walked to the door and slowly upstairs. He said:

"You see, Mary, the one weak spot in your father's confession is the statement that he stopped to get that theme. He says that he got it before going upstairs to kill Yerkes. He declares that he went into the building with the definite purpose of killing him; and yet, he says, by force of habit he stopped and opened the theme box. Mary, I can't believe he did that. That's why I want to see if the theme is here. If it is, his confession is consistent with the fact, but if it isn't—"

They went into her father's study. It seemed strangely dark and empty, as if some life had gone out of it, never to return. They stood before the desk, piled high with papers.

"It was a typewritten theme," Ingram said. "It was written in blue typewriter ink. The title, The Movement to Abolish the Death Penalty." As he said this he dared not meet her eyes.

He picked up a stack of papers and went through them carefully. She did the same with another heap. For more than half an hour they searched through the papers on top of the desk.

"Would it be in one of the drawers?" he queried.

For answer she opened a drawer and together they went through its contents. Then, methodically, carefully, they went through the contents of the others.

Abruptly Mary sat up. "I didn't think of it till now!" she said. "How stupid of me! Yesterday afternoon when Dad came in—it must have been when he came back from Chatham House—I helped him take off his coat. I recall now that he did seem upset. He said he had a headache and that he was going up to his study to lie down. I hung his topcoat on the rack downstairs. He got halfway up the stairs, then turned around and came down again, went to the topcoat and took something out of his pocket. It was a wad of crumpled or folded paper, I noticed, and he crushed it in his fist as he went upstairs again."

Ingram said: "Mary, we've got to find that wad of paper. If it means searching the whole house, we've got to find it. I wonder if he burned it. I wonder—"

He went hastily to the fireplace. The hearth was clean, dustless, ashless.

"He didn't burn it here," he said, and then went the round of the room, looking anxiously in all the ash trays. Then he looked about for a waste basket. There was none in the room.

"Where's the waste basket? He kept one here under the desk, didn't he?"

"Yes, he did. Probably Annie—"

"You ask Annie about that. And ask her if she cleaned up any ashes—paper ashes—out of any fireplace or ash tray or waste basket—out of any place at all in the house. Ask her that, will you?"

Mary went out quickly. Ingram sat at the desk and pondered the futility of the search. If they found the theme, it merely verified the confession. If they did not find it, nothing was proved, for he might have had it and done away with it.

Minutes went by. Then Mary came in excitedly.

"Ben!" she cried, "I've found it. I'm sure I have. It's in blue typewriter ink. It was in the basket in the back hall, torn to pieces. And here! Here's a piece that says Guido Luciano!"

She came forward with a handful of torn bits of paper. She laid them on the desk.

"Annie had left the waste baskets in the back hall unemptied. These scraps were in the basket from this room. Shall we try to put them together?"

Ingram fingered the bits of paper idly. "I don't know," he said. "Now that we've got it, it doesn't seem to help us any. It only proves that he did get the paper as he said he did."

He picked up one bit that bore some penciled figures. There were jerky, trembling numerals and two letters: "—rk 3287."

Ingram looked up. "Isn't that your father's handwriting?"

Mary examined the writing. "Well—yes. It seems so. But it's so jerky and uneven."

"As if," Ingram added, "his hand was trembling violently when he wrote it."

Mary met his eyes. "Yes. I think you're right. What does it mean?"

"I don't know. Let's see if we can find the rest of it."

He continued briefly to study the penciled marks. They had been written with a black lead but in the lines lay a faint hint of a metallic blue. Ingram touched a finger to his tongue and then to the figure

The "7" smeared slightly and became a distinct blue.

"Indelible pencil," Ingram said. He looked at the tray at the back of the desk, picked up the bunch of pencils there and examined them. Shaking his head, he replaced them. "Would you know if your father carried an indelible pencil?"

"I didn't know that he did," Mary said.

Frowning at the little scraps of paper before him, Ingram reflected that the note Yerkes had left him yesterday, Yerkes's last communication to him, had been written with this kind of lead.

"Yerkes used an indelible pencil," he murmured. "I know."

Mary glanced up quickly from the desk. "Does that mean that Father was with him when he wrote this—these figures? It means, then, that he did go up to see Philip Yerkes after taking the theme out of the box."

There was renewed pain in her eyes and the sight of it was misery for Ingram. He said: "Probably. Probably not. It may not mean a thing. Let's see if we can find the rest of what he wrote."

"Here!" Mary said after an interval. She pushed forward another bit of paper. Ingram picked it up. On one side were typewritten letters; on the other, in the same bluish-black lead, in the same nervous, jerking hand, was scrawled: "Glen Pa—"

"Glen Park," Mary said. "Glen Park 3287. Somebody's telephone number."

Ingram placed the two pieces together.

"Did you ever see or hear it before?" he asked.

"Not that I recall."

Ingram sat back, musing. In line with Bailey's confession, it was only too likely that he had written that number in Yerkes's office with Yerkes's pencil. The weight of this discouragement dragged his heart deeper into gloom.

He looked up at Mary. Her eyes were fixed intently on him, dark now with fear. . . .

This telephone number . . . it had come up between Bailey and Yerkes in a moment when Bailey was in great stress. . . .

Ingram reached for the telephone on Bailey's desk. "I'm going to get the listing of that number," he declared.

Leaning forward anxiously, Mary waited.

# 26
## THURSDAY 7:45 P.M.

Captain Packer ate his dinner, got into the police car and drove out to Chatham House.

There would be no one there now except a single officer on duty to keep out nosey people who might want to come in and poke about, do a little private detective work of their own or get souvenirs of the case.

The pale, insufficient yellow light in the lower corridor fell upon the sleepy-eyed patrolman who opened the door for him.

"Hello," the captain greeted. "All alone?"

"Yes, sir. Mr. Mortimer went away an hour ago. He said he'd be back pretty soon."

The captain went across the corridor to Ingram's office. The door stood open. Packer fumbled about for the wall button and snapped on the light. He seated himself at the desk, took out his pipe, loaded it, lighted up and puffed slowly, staring at the wall.

Carefully, after a brief interval, he pressed down the glowing tobacco with the end of his fountain pen. Funny business, this. Take it from the beginning.

Here's this Ingram. You'd say he was honest as the day was long. You'd say that whatever he told was so, and that was that. Giant of a feller. Think he played football here some years ago. Ingram. Yes. That's the bird. He was a guard, or a tackle. Seemed like the kind of man you could believe, taking his story just as he gave it. . . . Trouble was, there were sometimes you couldn't really believe anybody—not one hundred percent.

161

Now, Ingram comes over to this place here, meets the student, Luciano, coming away. Luciano has heard Yerkes's voice up here while he's putting the theme in the box. About a minute passes between the time Luciano leaves here and Ingram gets here. The shot is fired during that time. That puts Ingram pretty close to the building. You'd think, dammit, he'd have heard the shot.

But he's the kind of man gets thinking about things and wouldn't know if the whole world came piling down around him. For instance, last night when we went down street for a bite just before we went to Bailey's house the first time. Six different times I spoke to him and he didn't hear me. In the restaurant there. Just sat there, chewing away, forehead all wrinkled up. He was so far away in his thoughts I might have been talking to myself. Sociable enough when he snapped out of it. But he certainly had something on his mind. Wonder if he knows anything he's holding back. I think he'd play ball for those two if he had a chance. For Bailey anyhow. There's the girl.

Well, say he didn't hear the shot. Say he was that deep in his thinking. Now, he comes into the place; into his office here, closes the door and sits down at the desk.

In the meantime, Bailey and Davis are out there, out back. Now, I wonder did Ingram see them. You sit at this desk and you can look out the window and spot anybody going through there. Of course, maybe he didn't look out. But then, maybe he did. There's always the girl. When it's the girl's old man, I guess you don't see anything. Nice girl, that, too.

Hmph! Well, we've got 'em anyway. Bailey, at least. But I wonder if Ingram knows where Davis is. He might. Dear friend of the family, they tell me. I wonder. I think it wouldn't be a bad idea to put a tail on that feller, just to see where he goes. Maybe I'll do that.

The outer door across the corridor opened and Johnny Mortimer came in.

"Hello, captain. Anything new?"

"Nothing much."

"What about the bullet they fired at Luciano? What did the ballistics man say?"

Packer shook his head. "It didn't come from the same gun that killed Yerkes. And we've had the one that killed Crane since this morning. It's a third gun."

Mortimer sat down and thought it over. Then he asked: "Any news on that—what's his name?—Jerry the Pole; the one Thaddeus Davis met and walked away with?"

"Not a thing. He's gone. Nobody knows where he is. He's got a sister-in-law he lives with. She says she never knows where he goes nor when he's coming back."

"What about the Pole? Is he tied up with any outfit—Corvetti, for instance?"

"Hard to say. I don't think he's a Corvetti man. About four years ago here, somebody gave the Pole a dose of lead in the back. There was a general hunch that it was ordered from the Corvetti headquarters, but nobody ever proved anything. When the Pole pulled through—he's got the strength of an ox—he wouldn't say who did it. All he said was, how could he know who shot him if they came up behind? But I guess he knew all right. As a matter of fact, it was my idea at the time that Corvetti did know something about it. I went down and talked with him. He gave me the old song and dance. Didn't know anything about it. And we had nothing on anybody, so nothing happened."

The telephone rang. The captain reached for it. "Hello. Captain Packer talking."

"Hello, captain. This is Jennings. Over at the Davis place. Davis just showed up. I've got him here now. What do I do?"

The captain hollered: "Do? Just entertain him. I'll be over in five minutes." He hung up and faced Mortimer. "It's Davis. Jennings has got him over at his house. Let's go!"

"Can't," Mortimer declined. "I'm expecting a call from Bloomingdale. Are you bringing him back here?"

"No. Taking him right down to headquarters. See you later." He got up hastily, grabbed his hat and hurried out of the office, into Chatham Lane. At a long-legged stride he made for the police car, climbed in behind the wheel and sent the machine flying down Paisley Road.

So we've got you, my fine professor! I suppose you tried to sneak in, now that it's a little dark. You'll have to play a smarter game than that. You college profs—you think you've got all the brains and there was none left over for anyone else. Just wait till we get you talking. When we get your story and put two and two together, we'll have the right answer or I'm no judge.

He swung the car into North Park, shot past Price Street, and, two blocks further, swerved sharply into the street where Davis lived. The street, dimly lighted, sprang up in the brilliant headlights. The captain ran the car up to the curb, stopped it with a jerk and stepped out.

There were lights in the downstairs room on the left, the living room, as the captain remembered it.

There was also a dim light in one of the upstairs rooms. The shades in the downstairs room were raised. Packer could see Jennings standing with his back to the window, hands clasped behind him. Jennings was in plain clothes. He had relieved Maguire this afternoon. Davis, the captain could see from the verandah, was seated in a large armchair, reading a book. Pretty cool. The captain stabbed at the bell. Jennings started forward from the window and in a moment opened the door.

"He's in there," he said. "Reading a book, no less. Cool as a cucumber."

"What did he say when you took him? Where'd you take him anyway?"

"I was across the street, standing by a tree," Jennings said. "He came walking up the street. Not dodging. Not skulking. Just swinging along as if everything was fine. I wasn't even sure it was him. He turned in here and came up the steps and stopped to take out his key. I got to him before he got the door open. 'Are you Professor Davis?' I asks him. 'Yes,' he says. 'What can I do for you?' So I told him he was under arrest and when I told him what for he said it was a lot of nonsense but if we'd made up our minds to arrest him, why, all right. He asked as a special favor that I shouldn't say anything to his wife. She's upstairs lying down with a headache. He went up to see her for a few minutes and then came down and now he's been sitting there reading his book as calm as you please."

The captain walked past Jennings and into the living room. The professor glanced up. He looked neither upset nor worried. He set the book in his lap.

"Good evening, captain. Your man tells me I'm under arrest. I had scarcely expected anything like this, though I suppose it's your duty to make an arrest here and there on general principles." He smiled. "Have a seat. I must ask you to be very quiet. Mrs. Davis is lying down and I don't want her to be disturbed."

The captain made no move to seat himself. "Been looking for you all day, professor. We had an idea you were hiding out."

"Oh, no! Just a matter of business that kept me away. If I had known you were looking for me, I'd have come to see you at once."

Business, all right. Business with Jerry the Pole. The captain asked: "Know a man named Jerry the Pole, professor? Jerry Kameto?"

The professor gave no sign of surprise. Placidly, reflectively, he repeated the name. "Jerry Kameto? Jerry the Pole? No, I can't say that I do. Who is he?"

"It doesn't matter. I suppose you've been too busy to see the afternoon papers, professor?"

"As a matter of fact, I have."

"Then you wouldn't know that we've already arrested Professor Bailey."

"Good heavens!" Davis exclaimed. "When you police can't find a guilty person to arrest, is it imperative that you arrest an innocent one? Is that your duty to the public?"

"It's not a frame," the captain stated patiently. "You needn't stall any longer, professor. We know about your little episode at Chatham House at the time of the murder."

Davis demanded a little indignantly: "May I ask just what you mean?"

"Certainly. In the first place, Schultz, the janitor saw you leave there with Bailey, by the back door. What about that, professor?"

"I don't know what you're talking about. Schultz is lying."

"Oh, no, he isn't," Packer retorted. "We have Bailey's verification of it."

For several seconds Davis was silent, his eyes searching Captain Packer's face. "I don't believe that, captain."

The captain shrugged. "What you believe doesn't matter now. Bailey's made a full confession."

"A full confession?" Davis echoed slowly. "What do you mean?"

"In good time, you'll know what I mean. I haven't much time, right now, professor, so I'll ask you to come along with me."

Davis made a gesture of helplessness.

"I'm being arrested for murder?" he asked.

"It's a murder warrant."

"This is a great mistake, captain."

"Probably. We make mistakes now and then."

"I sincerely hope you rectify them." The professor's glance lingered now on the open book in his lap. Packer saw that it was poetry; a single stanza in the center of a page. On the opposite page was a picture; a picture of a young man sitting beside a girl in a wood.

Davis got up, laid aside the book.

"Tell me," he asked quietly, "when you say Professor Bailey made a full confession, do I understand you to mean that he has confessed to the murder of Philip Yerkes?"

The captain scanned the grave face intently. "That's exactly what I mean," he said.

Davis's eyes dropped and his hands came nervously together, the first indication that he was not as calm as he had been pretending to be.

"I—I'd like to go upstairs and say good-by to my wife," he said. "May I?"

The captain considered. "Bailey went out of the room to get his hat. He took poison by mistake and we barely brought him around."

"I shan't take poison," Davis promised. "I've no reason to do so. Come along with me, if you like,"

"No. Go ahead. We'll wait here. Don't be too long."

The professor's face lighted with gratitude. "Thank you, captain. I appreciate this greatly."

He walked out, ignored Jennings who stood in the hall, and went quietly upstairs.

Peculiar man, this. . . . Packer went over and picked up the book Davis had been reading. Rubaiyat of Omar Khayyam. Edward Fitzgerald's Version. Idly the captain turned the leaves and came soon to the picture of the boy beside the girl in the wood. The captain was no lover of poetry and no judge of it, but he was no scoffer. Solemnly he read the lines on the page before him:

> *But see! The rising Moon of Heav'n again*
> *Looks for us, Sweet-heart, through the quivering*
>     *Plane:*
>   *How oft hereafter will she look*
> *Among those leaves—for one of us in vain!*

# 27
## THURSDAY 8:25 P.M.

Captain Packer waited nearly ten minutes. He went out into the hall where Jennings was. He scowled at his watch.

"He takes his time. I wonder—"

Suddenly he pocketed the watch and went swiftly up the stairs. He went directly to the room at the front of the house, where he had seen the light from the street. He knocked, received no answer, opened the door. A soft light in a wall bracket was going. On the other side of the room, sleeping quietly on a divan, with a comforter thrown over her, was Mrs. Davis.

The captain closed that door again, then went quickly down the hall, opening doors as he went, thrusting in his head, turning on lights. Then, hastening back to the head of the staircase, he called down to Jennings:

"Jennings, the man's gone! Find the back door—in a hurry! See if you think he's gone that way. I'm going over the rest of the house."

He hastened up another flight, flung open doors, called for Davis to come out.

A room at the back of the house opened and a light flooded into the hall. The captain swung about. A thin woman in a faded green kimono stood there.

"What do you want?" she demanded. "Who are you?"

"I'm the police!" Packer snapped. "I'm looking for Davis. Who are you?"

"I'm the housekeeper," the woman said. "I thought the other man was the police. I—"

"Never mind that!" Packer cut in. "Davis came upstairs ten minutes ago to say good-by to his wife. Do you know where he went?"

The woman's brow wrinkled. "Not ten minutes ago, he couldn't say good-by to his wife. She was asleep more than ten minutes ago. I gave her her sleeping powder early tonight. She didn't feel good. She had a bad headache, and when she had them the doctor said to give her a powder. She ain't very well and—"

The captain ran for the stairway. Downstairs, he found Jennings returning from a search of the first floor.

"No sign of him," Jennings said. "He maybe ducked out the back door. There's no sign that he did, but there's no sign that he didn't."

"There's sign enough that he did!" the captain cried. "And I let him right through my fingers These smooth-talking professors! Out the back door with you, Jennings. See if he's skulking out there! I'm going through this house with a fine-tooth comb. He may be in a closet. There's that chance. And if he isn't, he'll get the prettiest broadcasting in the history of this state. He won't get far. Step on it, Jennings! See if he's there!"

# 28
## THURSDAY 8:30 P.M.

Ingram stayed to dinner with Mary Bailey and I afterwards, when he went home, he telephoned the district attorney.

First he called Bloomingdale's home and was informed that the district attorney was still in his office. He then telephoned there.

"This is Ingram," he said. "I'm sorry to trouble you when I know you're so busy. But I wonder if you'd tell me something about—" He paused. He was asking for official information. He knew it was a presumption.

"Yes?" Bloomingdale urged. "I'm not too busy to talk with you. Go ahead. What do you want to know?"

"Well, I wanted to know if your fingerprint people found any of Bailey's prints in Yerkes's office?"

"Oh, yes," Bloomingdale replied. "Yes, indeed. We didn't know whose they were at first, but of course we know now. What about it?"

"Did you find any," Ingram pursued, "on a pencil on the desk?"

After a brief silence, Bloomingdale laughed. "Still sleuthing on your own? Just a minute." There was another silence. Then: "Yes, as a matter of fact, Bailey's prints were found on a pencil— among other things. Interested in what kind of pencil? Let's see. It's a yellow wooden pencil; no name of maker; it just says—oh, it says Indelible on it. Does that interest you? You aren't holding out on me, are you, professor?"

"I'm simply trying hard," Ingram told him, "to disprove Bailey's confession."

"Don't waste time doing that. You'd only upset my case if you did."

"That's what I'm trying to do."

"That's a stiff order, even for you, professor. It's open and shut now. Anything else?"

"I believe not. Thanks very much. Hope I haven't been a nuisance."

"Not at all. Never too busy to talk with you. Any time."

"Thanks. Good-by."

He hung up. The fact was definitely settled now. Bailey had written that telephone number on Luciano's theme while in Yerkes's office. Ingram sat at his desk, mustering his arguments, attempting to theorize in the confusion that lay about him.

For the purpose of keeping his arguments straight, he jotted them down on paper:

I. I do not believe that if Bailey went to Chatham House expressly to kill Yerkes, he would have stopped first to open the theme box and take out that theme. And yet the telephone number written in Bailey's hand with a pencil from Yerkes's desk shows that Bailey did have that theme before he went to do his confessed killing.

II. It is logical to assume, therefore, that he did not come expressly to kill Yerkes.

III. If he did not come expressly to kill Yerkes, he would have entered by the front door of Chatham House.

IV. Assuming he entered by the front door: To get the theme before killing Yerkes, he must have entered Chatham House between the time Luciano left and I arrived.

V. *He did not enter Chatham House during this interval*, for had he done so, I should have seen him: The front door of Chatham House was in full view to me from the moment Luciano stepped out.

VI. If he did not enter by the front door during this interval, it is possible that he came by the rear door. This use of the rear door would indicate a guilty intent. But the intent and the taking of the theme paper are not consistent. I am not sure that he did enter by the rear door. I am sure that he took out the theme. Ergo, it is fair to assume that he had no guilty intent at the time of taking the theme. Ergo, he did not enter by the rear door.

VI. This leaves but one theory consistent with the above: *Bailey was in the building before Luciano deposited the theme.*

VIII. Assuming, now, that he was in the building, that he was in Yerkes's office, that Davis was there too, that it was their voices Luciano had heard: did Bailey, during the single minute between Luciano's departure and my entrance, go downstairs, open the theme box, get the theme, rush upstairs again to Yerkes's office, write down that telephone number, kill Yerkes, and then hasten away downstairs with Davis? Or did Bailey leave Davis in quarrel with Yerkes and go downstairs to the theme box; did Davis kill Yerkes in that brief interval; did Bailey rush upstairs to see what had happened and, while there, pencil that telephone number and then go downstairs with Davis, into the basement? Could all this have taken place in a minute? It is possible, but is it probable? . . .

Ingram threw down his pencil. . . . That all important minute: His own entry marked the finish of it. Luciano's exit marked its beginning.

But why—and the thought, from far back in Ingram's mind pounded its way to the fore with ever-increasing persistence— why did everyone take Luciano's word so implicitly? Why might there not be something that the student was hiding?

Why might it not be that he was lying outright? But if he was lying, in what did his lie consist? And what was the reason for it? And in what way were Bailey and Davis involved in that lie? And why should Bailey make verification of such a lie?

What was it all about? What was the truth behind all this?

Floundering hopelessly, sick at heart, Ingram walked his floor. The facts swarmed about him, confused him horribly. He sorted them out and they flew away again into an untidy disorder before he could muster, arrange and make deductions from them.

He was very tired. His brain needed rest even more than his limbs. Yet he knew that he could not sleep.

He went to the door and called through the house for his housekeeper. She came quickly, silent in soft slippers, blinking over reading glasses.

"Yes, professor?"

"Bring me some coffee, please. Black. Strong. Strong as you can make it, please."

She smiled. "Yes, professor." She went away.

Ingram sat down in an armchair. It was nine o'clock. At ten he must see Blanding, the Coombs executor.

# 29
## THURSDAY 9:35 P.M.

Shortly after nine-thirty Ingram started for town. He had plenty of time to get there, so he drove slowly, refreshing himself in the cool night air.

He did not know Blanding, but the man had seemed willing enough to talk about the Coombs matter, even though he did not know yet just what angle of it Ingram wanted to discuss. It was quite possible that he would refuse to cooperate. After all, there was nothing definite that Ingram could ask for. He wanted to know if there had been anything in Coombs's effects which might in some way give a clue in Coombs's decease and, per-chance, in Yerkes's and Crane's.

Likely enough it was a futile errand, probably a search in things quite remote from the matters in hand, but Ingram felt that here was a stone that should not be left unturned.

Before the building in which Blanding had his office, Ingram parked the car. The building was mostly dark. Here and there shone a light in a window. There were lights in the entrance and in the corridor. The elevators were not running. Ingram consult-ed the building directory and went up to the third floor. Number 352 was Blanding's. The inscription on the door said: "Anthony Blanding. Attorney at Law. Walk in."

Ingram went in. There was an outer office, which was dark. However, the door to a room at the far end was open and a light streamed out.

Ingram went to that door. "Good evening," he greeted. "Mr. Blanding?"

A slender, frail white-haired old man sat at a large desk, facing the door. He looked up and Ingram saw very blue eyes in a wrinkled face.

The old man laid down a pen and got up from his chair.

"Good evening. Professor Ingram?"

They shook hands. Ingram said: "You work late."

"Have for years. Sleep little and work late. Habit, I suppose. Sit down, professor. Have a cigar and tell me what it was you wanted to know about Coombs."

Ingram took the cigar and the proffered light.

"I hope you aren't going to think this an intrusion," he began. "I'm in pretty deadly earnest about this. The facts surrounding it are very serious."

Blanding nodded, lighting a cigar for himself. Ingram went on: "In the first place, yesterday afternoon Professor Philip Yerkes was murdered out at the university. You read about it?"

"Yes. I was shocked. I had met Yerkes. He was a fine man."

"Well," Ingram continued, "we've been in quite a turmoil over there, what with the second murder—the student, Crane— and the arrest of Professor Bailey and his confession, and so on. I'm intensely concerned with all these things, Mr. Blanding. In the first place, Yerkes was a very good friend of mine. So is Professor Bailey. I'd do anything in my power to get at the truth in all this. The police are trying, I know, but I'm impelled irresistibly to seek out certain things for my own satisfaction. I don't know what they'll mean when I find them. But find them I must. And I've come here tonight to ask you to help me. I've little or no right at all to ask, and I certainly shan't hold it against you if you simply say it can't be done and send me on my way."

Blanding puffed on his cigar, stroked his wrinkled chin and said: "I'm not going to send you away, professor. I'm intensely interested too. Just how can I help you?"

Ingram leaned forward to present the gist of his case.

"It's my opinion," he declared, "that Yerkes was investigating the death of—"

"Professor Coombs?" Blanding put in softly. "He thought that Coombs had been murdered, had discovered the murderer and was himself murdered because he knew?"

Ingram stared. "How did you know that?"

Blanding explained: "Yerkes came to see me a while ago. He wanted probably the very thing that you want. He wanted to go through Coombs's papers for some form of evidence to prove that Coombs had been murdered. I permitted him to do so."

"And what did he find?"

Blanding shrugged. "I don't know exactly. I certainly had found nothing that looked like a clue, and of course I had been through his papers quite thoroughly. But then, I'm not much of a detective. Yerkes jotted down notes from several papers. I asked him if he had found anything of importance. He said he didn't know. Said he wasn't sure. He consulted me about several of the papers. I explained their import as well as I could. As a matter of fact, I believe there was only one that I couldn't give a fair explanation of. He copied that one verbatim and then he went away and I never saw him again after that."

"How long ago was this?"

"Oh—two months. Probably a little more."

Ingram smoked his cigar, watching the blue smoke curl gracefully away. "Then it's not unlikely that something Yerkes found here led him to what he wanted to know—and so to his death."

"It is not unlikely."

Eagerly intent, Ingram leaned forward again and put a great fist on Blanding's desk.

"Mr. Blanding," he said, "I want to go through those papers, if I may."

Blanding shrugged. "If you're really looking for trouble as much as that," he agreed.

At midnight they came across the paper that Blanding had been unable to explain to Yerkes.

"This was the one," Blanding said. "I haven't the faintest idea what it may mean. It may be a money accounting. I don't know. It didn't seem to come into the picture when the estate was wound up. It didn't seem—"

Ingram heard no more that Blanding was saying. He was scanning the paper carefully and with scarcely concealed excitement.

There were two rows of figures. They ran: 100, 250, 100, 500, 100, 300—and so on. The figures of themselves were not exciting, but the jotting at the foot of the page was. Ingram could scarcely believe his eyes. This, then, did mean something. It had meant something in Coombs's life as well as in Bailey's.

"What's this?" Ingram asked, putting a finger on it. "What did this mean to Coombs? Have you any idea?"

Blanding picked up the paper and examined the jotting.

"Whose handwriting is it?" Ingram asked.

"Oh, the handwriting is Coombs's right enough, but what it means I don't know. Think it's important? Does it mean anything to you?"

"Not yet," Ingram replied. "It may soon. We'll see."

Blanding sat with the paper in his hand. "Might be a telephone number," he suggested. "G. P. 3287. Might be Glen Park. Why not? Glen Park 3287. Would that mean anything to you?"

# 30
## FRIDAY 8 A.M.

Ingram spent a restless night. During part of it he dozed, awakening now and then with a horrible start from a ghastly nightmare. During the rest of it he walked the floor, scuffing back and forth between the windows and the far wall, pausing at the windows to look out and down upon the calm, whispering trees.

It was a night of somber stillness and the moonlight was like a chill metallic reflection. Ingram had looked down upon this stillness before and found it sweet and the moonlight soft, warm, friendly. Not so tonight. The silence was heavy not with peace but with a thick mystery, and the moonlight was like the cold gray light that had fallen across the floor in Bailey's cell yesterday afternoon.

Turning away from the window, his body weary but his mind active with bloated night fears, Ingram got into bed for perhaps the tenth time and lay awake staring at the dark ceiling; desperately worried, unable to shake off the black apprehension; unable to blot out the image of an enormous, dark circular wall of law and tragedy that had sprung up about Hardwick Bailey, now closing in upon him, a little at a time, eventually to squeeze, to grind, to crush him into nothing.

His father's friend. One of the dearest of his own. Father of the woman he loved. Locked in a gray-black cell. Nodding blankly at accusations of murder. . . .

And Thaddeus Davis. . . . Missing. Hunted. And probably, by morning, shouted after from one end of the country to the

179

other. . . . Ingram tossed and turned, and after a while the darkness paled, the moon faded and the gray morning came. And soon the sun came out, bright and warm, and crept across the room, and for a little while Ben Ingram fell into a deep sleep, until his alarm clock wakened him suddenly.

He stood under the shower until he felt relieved a little of his dragging fatigue. He dressed slowly, then telephoned to his assistant and asked him to take over his classes as he had done the day before. Then he went down to breakfast and, finding no morning paper beside his plate, called for Mrs. Eagan.

She came in, eyes fixed on him pityingly.

"Where's the paper?" he asked.

She hesitated. "Well, I didn't bring it in because I thought—Well, there's some upsetting news and I thought you ought to eat your breakfast first in peace and—"

"Please bring it, Mrs. Eagan."

"Promise you'll eat breakfast," she insisted.

"I'll eat it."

She went away and came back with the paper. He opened it. Headlines. Poor old Tad. Mrs. Eagan stood there uneasily.

"Eat your fruit," she said.

Absently he picked up his spoon.

The headlines:

## MURDER WARRANT
## FOR PROFESSOR DAVIS
### UNIVERSITY PROFESSOR ELUDES POLICE

Taken into custody last night, Professor Thaddeus Davis, eminent University faculty member, gave the slip to his captors and is at present at large. Arrested at his home, Professor Davis requested permission to say good-by to his wife, left the officers waiting in his living room and failed to return. The officers, in charge of Captain Samuel Packer, Chief of the Homicide Squad, searched the house. Davis had vanished, presumably by the rear door. The combined police forces of the entire state have flung out a network which, it is predicted, will effect an early capture.

The police promise startling revelations in the murder cases of Professor Philip Yerkes and the student Leonard Crane. District Attorney Bloomingdale late last night made the statement that the case was well in hand and promised a speedy trial.

. . .

Wearily Ingram read the repetitious details, slowly consuming his breakfast, for which he now had less appetite than before.

He finished in complete gloom and at length left the house, drove out his car and headed for the city. He was going to learn this morning what Glen Park 3287 might mean. . . .

The listing operator had given him the name and address of the person whose telephone it was. The name was Maybelle Cunningham, the address one at the far side of the city. It was Ingram's resolve to find out in what way Maybelle Cunningham was concerned in the affairs of Professor Coombs and Professor Bailey.

Grimly he drove to Maybelle Cunningham's address.

The street was a wide, riverside drive and the houses along the way were imposing apartment groups. Ingram drew up before the number he sought, got out, strolled up the walk to the steps, went into the vestibule.

He looked in vain for mail boxes and the names of the tenants. They must be in the inner vestibule. He pushed open a heavy door and walked in. At the left of the door here he found mail boxes, but there were no names. He glanced down the hall to what seemed to be a small office and in which a uniformed attendant was sitting.

As he approached, the attendant got up quickly, opened the glass door of the office and stepped out. He was a young Irishman, blond, cheerful-faced.

"May I help you? Are you looking for someone?"

"Yes," Ingram began. And then the young man stepped forward with an exclamation of recognition and pleasure. He proceeded to take Ingram's hand and pump it up and down.

"Hello, professor! Gosh! Imagine seeing you here! Remember me? I'm Michael Flynn. You remember me! I used to caddy for you over at Peacebrook—five years ago."

"Oh, yes," Ingram said. "Hello, Michael. I'm glad to see you. Do you own this apartment house now?"

Michael laughed. "No," he said. "No. Say, I'm just a sort of superintendent. Also a watch dog. It's a very snooty place, this. I only let in the ones that look as if they ought to be let in and then only when the tenants say they want them in. And besides, I see that everything keeps going smooth in the whole block— janitors and like that."

"Pretty responsible job for a young fellow," Ingram smiled.

"Sure!" the youth exclaimed. "And if you think I didn't get it through pull, you've got another guess. They usually give it to an older man. But you didn't come down here to chew the fat with me, professor. Who'd you want to see?"

Ingram hesitated. "The first one I want to see—really, Michael—is you. May I come into your office and have a talk?"

"Gosh!" cried Michael. "Sure! Come in! It's an honor, professor. Anything special you want to talk about?"

Michael closed the door. Ingram seated himself in a chair beside Michael's desk. He could see down the vestibule to the elevators and past these to the outer vestibule and the street.

"I don't know, Michael," he began, "whether I have any business asking you about this. Frankly, I want to find out something about a tenant of yours and—"

Michael waved a hand. "Go ahead, professor. Ask me anything you like. I'll even tell you what they have for breakfast or"—and he winked—"for midnight snacks. To anybody else it's strictly confidential—but to you, professor, it's an open book. I'm not forgetting in a long time how white you treated me at Peacebrook. Go ahead, professor. The sky's the limit. Who do you want the dirt on?"

Ingram smiled soberly. "It's good of you, Michael, and thanks. Briefly, I want to find out what I can about a certain Maybelle Cunningham of this address."

Michael's eyebrows went up.

"Maybelle Cunningham!" he repeated. He smiled for an instant and then his face went grave. "Just what do you want to know about her?"

"Whatever you can tell me."

"You know who she is, don't you—or do you?" Michael asked.

"I don't know a thing about her."

"Well, she's a—well—this is strictly confidential, professor—she's a sort of flashy dame. Has an apartment upstairs on the fifth floor, rear. She's a young dame, about twenty-two, maybe twenty-three. Good looker. Swell looker. And—" Michael paused, glanced through the glass door, then continued "—and she's got a boyfriend."

He paused, his glance indicating that his last statement was weighty, significant. "Know who the boyfriend is?" he asked.

"No."

"Ever hear of Joe Corvetti?"

"Yes. I believe I've read about him in the papers now and then. He's a gangster, isn't he?"

"Isn't he!" Michael echoed. "He's *the* gangster. He's the real well-known Public Enemy, without any number attached to him. All the others are Public Enemy No. 1 or 2 or 3 and so on. This guy ain't got a number. He's the big top one—ahead of all the numbers. They say he's got a gang of about fifteen, and those fifteen do all the operating for him. Nobody else sticks a nose in, they say. Say, he's got a sort of corporation, and all the fifteen are share holders. They have board meetings and plan big stuff and go straight through with it. Nothing small time about them. They were in the bootleg business before repeal sneaked up on them. Now I hear they're in dope and kidnapping and this business-protective stuff and anything else you can think of that there's a dirty dollar in."

"And this woman?" Ingram asked.

"Well, as I say, she's the girlfriend—Corvetti's. Snappy number, professor. And they say she's nuts about Corvetti. He's got one of the biggest apartments in the place for her up there. And is it swell! Like you see in the movies. Say, they've even got their own telephone system in there. Private lines and that kind of thing. For instance, Corvetti's got his business quarters down-town. Now, they say there's more than one way to get in touch with those quarters by phone. But one of the ways is to call up Maybelle and ask to be put through. Maybelle plugs in a switch and it connects the outside call with Corvetti at his headquarters. Then they have—"

He stopped. Ingram heard the soft whirr of the elevator mechanism out in the vestibule.

"Just a minute," said Michael. "Maybe this is—"

The elevator came softly to rest at the vestibule level and its door opened and a woman stepped out. She was tall, exquisite, red-lipped, blonde, gorgeously dressed.

"There's your Maybelle!" Michael whispered.

Behind her came a man. A tall, dark man. His skin was olive colored, the eyes dark and sharp. He did not turn and look into the office, nor did Maybelle; but Ingram had a glance that was sufficient. He sat forward with a little start, staring not at Maybelle but at her escort.

Michael was whispering something, but Ingram did not hear. He was gazing after the man with Maybelle. The two went out, down the steps and out of sight. Michael whispered on, but still Ingram did not hear.

He was recalling suddenly the meeting of District Attorney Bloomingdale with Guido Luciano, two days ago at Chatham House.

"You're Luciano—Guido Luciano?" Bloomingdale had said with a little frown. "Look here, Luciano, where have I seen you before?"

And Luciano had answered calmly: "I don't know."

Bloomingdale had said: "I get it. You remind me of someone. Who would it be?"

Calmly again Luciano had made reply: "I don't know."

But Ingram knew now. He knew now why Luciano's face had been familiar to Bloomingdale. He knew now why Bloomingdale's face had puckered up in an effort to recall—to put two with two. He knew now where Bloomingdale had seen a face that was like Luciano's.

It was as if a rocket had burst in a black night, flinging light upon figures that lurked in the dark.

Michael was whispering.

"Yes, sir! The gent with Maybelle is Joe Corvetti, king of the gangsters! Take a good look, professor. He's the biggest Big Shot there is!"

# 31
## FRIDAY 11 A.M.

It was with an intense excitement that Ingram drove back to the university. He went directly to his home and immediately to the telephone and called the district attorney.

They told him that Mr. Bloomingdale was out of the office and could not be reached on the telephone for the present and would probably not return until the afternoon.

Ingram then tried to get in touch with Captain Packer. The captain likewise was unavailable. Ingram pushed aside the telephone and sat wringing his hands in disturbed thought.

Why, this could mean anything! Anything at all. And the bottom of it must be fathomed before more sinister, terrible things happened. Why, every one had the wrong slant on the entire matter. There was more behind it—a vast unbelievable machinery of crime—than anyone would have believed.

The first thing to do, and no doubt about this at all, was to get in touch with Luciano. Luciano was a liar. He must know more than he had told, and likely enough he had lied about what he had told.

Ingram got hastily to his feet. If he couldn't get in touch with Bloomingdale or Packer, he would handle the matter himself. On second thought, it was perhaps best that he handle it himself anyway. If the matter was as deeply involved as this, there was no knowing how securely established spies might be; to what extent the police themselves might be on a gangster's payroll.

Yes, the best thing to do was to handle the matter himself. No paid spies would know where he was going nor what he was doing. No one in his confidence would betray him because he would take no one into his confidence. Why, he could get the truth quickly now—and get it he would.

He snatched his hat from the hall rack and went out. He got into his car and drove east toward the dormitories, getting the better of his inner excitement as he went, calming himself with the thought that he would need and must have a calm, a cool head.

He drew up outside the dormitory, went in and sought the rooms occupied by Luciano. Several students, coming and going, nodded respectfully, and some turned and gazed after him as he went swiftly past down the corridor.

He knocked at Luciano's door. There was no answer. He knocked again. Still no answer. He laid hold of the knob and tried the door. It was locked.

A tall red-haired student came up. "Looking for Luciano, sir? I saw him go out of there about an hour ago. Can I take a message for him? I'll probably see him later in the morning. He's in my twelve o'clock class."

"No, thanks," Ingram replied. "It's not necessary to tell him I was looking for him. I'll have the office take care of what I wanted."

He went down the corridor and out of the building, and the red-haired student looked after him with furrowed brow.

Ingram drove home. A police car stood outside his door. He parked behind it and went in. In his living room he found Mrs. Eagan standing before Bloomingdale and Captain Packer. Mrs. Eagan was belligerent and tearful. She turned with a little cry to Ingram as he entered.

"Oh, professor!" she cried. "Will you get these police to let me alone! They've come in here and they've been asking me questions like I was a murderer myself—and like you was one too. And I've told them—"

"Just a minute," Ingram said. "Bloomingdale, what's this all about?"

Bloomingdale shrugged. "We're hunting for a fugitive from justice, professor," he said. "One never knows where he'll find such a man."

"You mean," Ingram retorted in quick anger, "that you think Davis is here—that he's hiding in this house? Well, if you think he is, why don't you get a search warrant and look? For that matter, you're welcome to look without a warrant."

"Thanks," said Bloomingdale. "We've the search warrant already. But we didn't come here merely to look in your closets. What we want to do is talk with you."

"Seems to me," Ingram told him, "you might have done that without going out of your way to annoy my housekeeper. Mrs. Eagan, if these gentlemen are through bullying you, why don't you go upstairs and lie down. Everything will be all right. Run along."

Sniffing, Mrs. Eagan cast a hurt, hostile glance at Bloomingdale and Packer and went out.

Ingram said: "Well, what is it? I'm prepared to answer any questions you want to ask."

Bloomingdale said placatingly: "Now, Ingram, it won't do any one any good to get angry. I assure you we want to do this in a nice peaceful way, if we can. But you must realize, man, that we've got a very vital job on our hands, and I guess you know we mean business. We're looking for Davis, and—"

"And you think I'm harboring him?" Ingram demanded warmly.

"Well—"

"Well, let me tell you something, Bloomingdale, and you too, Packer. As a matter of fact, I'm not harboring him. I haven't the faintest idea where he is. But I'll tell you this: If I did know where he was and had a chance to help him, I'd most certainly do so. And do you know why? Because that man's innocent. He's as innocent as you are. He's a good man. I know him. I've known him too long. I've—"

"Please!" Bloomingdale interjected. "We know how you feel about him. It's too bad it all had to happen, but we can't ignore facts just because you two were good friends. The fact remains—doesn't it?—that he made a very deliberate escape from arrest. I don't know how you're going to reconcile that with your idea that he's an innocent man. If he were innocent, Ingram, he'd come in and tell what he knows. But he's run away. And we can't lay hands on him. To tell the truth, we did have an idea you probably knew where he was and we came over to ask you to listen to reason. And why? Because you can't afford, Ingram, to tie up with criminals—no matter how long or deep the friendship. Of course, if you say now that you don't know where he is and haven't helped him to get away, why, of course we take your word. The last thing we want to do, professor, is to antagonize you. But the captain and I are trying to do our duty as we see it, and there's no stone we're going to leave unturned. I take it, then, your last word on this is that you don't know where Davis is, don't know where he's going to be, and haven't helped him to make this get-away. Is that right? Do I have your word on it?"

"That's right," Ingram said. "You have my word. I haven't any idea of his whereabouts, and I had nothing to do with his escape last night. I knew nothing about it until I read the story in the paper this morning."

"Very well," said Bloomingdale. "Sorry."

He went to the door and Packer followed, nodding briefly to Ingram. They went out and Ingram stood at the door, looking after them.

They got into the police car, Packer behind the wheel.

"Well, what do you think?" Packer asked.

"Think!" Bloomingdale exclaimed. "Damned if I know what to think. Put a man on that fellow's tail right away, captain, will you? I want to know every move he makes from now on."

# 32
## THE PREVIOUS NIGHT—THURSDAY 10 P.M.

Professor Thaddeus Davis moved with unhurried step across the open field. There was plenty of moonlight for him to see or to be seen if anyone was looking for him. It was an unusually still and beautiful night. The moonlight cast sharply the shadows of the buildings at the far end of the field. The professor walked on until he came to the corner of one of these buildings, walked around that corner into a dark areaway and here halted, looking at the black object that stood hunched against one of the walls.

The black object was a car. A voice from the car said: "Is that you, professor?"

The professor started forward once more and came to the side of the car. It was a big sedan. The man at the wheel peered at him, as if to reassure himself.

"Good evening, Jerry," the professor greeted. "Are we ready?"

"Yeah, we're ready. I thought you wasn't comin', professor. You're late about an hour."

"I know," the professor acknowledged. "It wasn't easy. I very nearly failed you entirely."

Jerry laughed. "Failed me! Failed yourself. This ain't exactly my party, professor. What happened?"

"I walked right into the hands of the police, Jerry. A man named Jennings and Captain Packer. Right in my own home."

"I told you so," Jerry said annoyedly. "I told you so, professor. What do you think cops are—a hundred percent dumb? Well, they ain't. They'd be spottin' your house if they wasn't spottin' any other place in the country. You shouldn't have gone back there."

191

"I told you, Jerry, I had to see Mrs. Davis."

"Well, you seen her now. Let's get goin'."

The professor did not yet move from the side of the car. He said: "I saw her, Jerry, but she didn't see me. She was asleep."

"Whyn't you wake her up?"

"Well, you see, Jerry, she'd been having one of those bad headaches of hers and the maid had given her a sleeping powder. I didn't want to wake her up."

"If she was my wife and I wanted to see her," Jerry muttered, "I'd wake her up."

The professor smiled. "I don't think you would, Jerry."

Jerry the Pole made an exasperated sound. "Don't you know anything about dames at all?" he asked. "She'll be sore you didn't wake her. That's the way dames are. Professor, for a guy that's supposed to know as much as you, you don't know a hell of a lot—you know it?"

Still the professor smiled. "I suppose not. But then, I suppose I haven't had your experience with women, Jerry."

"That's right!" said Jerry. "Take me for a ride! Kid me along! This is a fine time for kiddin'. What are we stallin' around for, anyhow? We're supposed to be gettin' places. We'll get picked up if you don't look out."

"We're probably safer here than anywhere," the professor said. "And we certainly mustn't do any obvious hurrying. If we do, the chances are greater that we'll be picked up."

"Well, come on, anyhow. Let's get goin'. We got to get goin' some time, ain't we? The longer we stall, the longer we have to worry."

"Are you worried, Jerry?"

"Worried!" Jerry exploded. "Sure I'm worried! No, not about me. I'm worried about you, that's all."

The professor laid a hand on Jerry's arm. "Jerry," he said, "that touches me deeply." He went around the car and got in beside him. "Any time now, Jerry."

"Okay. Here goes." He turned on the lights, stepped on the starter. The car snorted, then began to purr softly. Jerry had an afterthought. "You know why I like you, professor?" he asked.

"No. Why do you like me?"

"Because you don't talk down to me. Because you're a big brain but you don't talk down to me. See?"

"Thanks, Jerry. Do you know why I like you?"

"No. Maybe no good reason."

"Because you don't talk up to me. I get tired of having people talk up to me—students and other people."

"I get it," Jerry grunted. "Because I'm a little brain but don't talk up to you."

"I didn't say that, Jerry. You know what I meant. I don't have to explain to you."

Jerry laughed. "You're right, professor. You don't have to explain anything to me. With me you're a hundred percent jake—comin' and goin'. If you wasn't, would I be here now with you?"

"I'm very grateful," the professor assured him.

"You damn well ought to be," Jerry said. "I'm a swell guy all right."

"Certainly you are. Shall we start now?"

Jerry ran the car slowly out of the areaway, across the field behind the building and then around a corner and out into a dark street.

"Not too fast, not too slow; that's us," Jerry said. "What was I sayin'—I'm a swell guy? Don't let that bother you, professor. I'm no dumb cluck. I just like to shoot my mouth. I always been that way. Always shootin' my mouth. Mouth shooters ain't any good anyway, professor. . . . You know, professor, you'd prob'ly have done your good deed for the day if you'd left me in the trench to have a bayonet for lunch instead of givin' me a piggie-back home. That was no job for a major anyhow. What was the matter with you—was you crazy?"

"No. Not that time. No. I knew what I was doing."

"Well, I'm glad you did it, professor; all kiddin' aside. I had some good times since then. Some bad ones, but some good ones too. I can't kick."

"Neither can I."

They went out of the dark street into another, even darker. They went by a circuitous route, seeming always to avoid main highways. They traveled a long while in complete silence.

The night grew deeper. At times the moon disappeared, but only briefly. It came out again and shone down on country roads. There was almost no traffic. They were unmolested by police. They did not so much as see a policeman. The professor sat grimly beside Jerry the Pole, peering sharp-eyed into the gloom ahead, one hand gripping the side of the car, at the open window.

Jerry spoke: "We're gonna be late. Somebody'll wait for us, though. They ought to know you can't travel this way on schedule."

"How much further?" the professor asked.

"Plenty."

For nearly an hour more they drove in renewed silence. Then the professor said: "Of course you know, Jerry, I appreciate very much the fact that you don't ask questions."

"Sure. I know all I need to know."

And there was silence again.

They came at length to the outskirts of a city. They went by way of narrow, winding streets, past dingy tenements and at last to a long, low brick building. Jerry ran the car into a small lot beside the building.

"Here's where we get out," he said. "Now, I don't know exactly who's gonna be here. The guy we met yesterday, Coober, said he couldn't wait long for us if we was late. Anyhow, someone'll be here. Here we go."

They got out of the car and went to a side door. Jerry knocked and the door was opened almost immediately.

"Hello," Jerry said. "Who's here?"

"I am," said the man. "Nelligan. Porky's inside. Coober couldn't wait. You're plenty late."

"I said maybe we'd be late," Jerry told him. "Come on in, professor."

They went down a narrow passageway and into a brilliantly lighted long room without windows. At the far end of the room, against the wall, were targets. There was a stationary bull's-eye, another on a swinging pendulum, and beside that was the figure of a man, done in black on the wall against a white background.

A man came to meet them at the door. He was a stout, smiling man with a cigar between his teeth. He shook hands with the professor. Nelligan went back down the passage.

"Hello," the stout man said. "Coober had to go. I'm the—the business manager. He gave me the story. He says you're okay if you've got the cash."

"I have the cash," the professor said. He took out a wallet and counted out a wad of bills. The stout man took the money, counted it, stuffed it into a pocket.

"Good guns are hard to get hold of these days," he declared. "That little arrangement with Corvetti ain't on the bill at all; ain't costing you a cent. Just between you and me, it's a favor to somebody around here. It's all fixed up. They're expecting you. They're having a board meeting tomorrow night—Friday—especially on this account. They want to see what the new gun acts like, and Corvetti says he's in the market for plenty of 'em if it's okay." He laughed. "He'll find it's okay."

The professor looked about. "Where's the gun?" he asked.

The stout man went to a desk in a corner and opened a suitcase that lay upon it.

"Here," he said. He lifted out a gleaming submachine gun. "Here you are. The lightest and best. Light as a feather. Heft it, professor. I'll bet you never saw anything like this in the war."

The professor took the gun out of his hands and examined it.

"She's all set," the stout man told him. "She's got a safety catch there. You just flip it. She's got a hair trigger—no strain on the finger. Just as long as you touch her—she talks. We call her the Featherbaby. Try her on the target."

The professor turned away to the range, lifted the gun and laid his finger on the trigger. The gun spat a stream of lead. The professor fanned it back and forth slightly. The swinging pendulum rang. The professor concentrated the fire on the figure of the man.

Then he stopped shooting. He handed the gun back to the stout man after examining it briefly again. "It's all right," he said. "It's very good."

"You bet it's very good." The stout man put the gun back into the suitcase, snapped it shut and put it on the floor. "All right now, professor. Everything's all set. They're expecting you. You're the agent. Just be cagey. Tell 'em we can let 'em have all they want of these within reason. Give 'em the old sales talk. Good luck."

"Thank you," said the professor.

"Give my love to Corvetti," the stout man said with a wink. "Tell him I'll be seeing him."

"I'll tell him," the professor nodded. He picked up the suitcase and walked out of the range room. The stout man nodded at Jerry the Pole.

"Some guy, that," he said.

"You're tellin' me?" said Jerry.

## 33
## FRIDAY 10 P.M.


Ingram laid his hand upon the knob of Luciano's door, found it unlatched, opened it, stepped in.

The study, alight, was empty, but Ingram could hear the sound of someone moving about in the bedroom at the left. Ingram stood silent just inside the door for a moment, the door still ajar. He was tense and in him surged a strange excitement of a kind that he had not experienced in years. Oddly enough, it was similar to the excitement he had known before going on to the gridiron years ago for an especially important game.

It was the third time he had been to Luciano's rooms that day. On both of the previous occasions the door had been locked and Luciano nowhere about. But this time the man was here, and the chat that Ingram meant to have with him was close at hand. Ingram closed the door silently, stood with his back to it, waiting.

In the bedroom, the door to which stood open, he heard the striking of a match and then Luciano's voice humming softly. In a moment, threads of blue-gray cigarette smoke drifted into the study. Motionless, Ingram waited.

The humming ceased and Luciano picked up the same tune in a soft whistle. Ingram heard the scuff of slippers. Luciano was approaching the door. But then the sound retreated again as he went away to the far end of the bedroom.

In a moment the whistle became brisker and louder. Luciano was heading for the study. Ingram stood facing the bedroom door.

Luciano came into the doorway and his whistling ceased abruptly. He stared, mouth open for a moment, at Professor Ben Ingram.

"Well!" he exclaimed. "This *is* a surprise!"

Ingram said nothing. Luciano remained in the doorway, looking at the professor with a poorly-concealed wariness. Then he broke out into a cheerful laugh.

"Well, after all, professor, now that you've been kind enough to come in to pay me a visit—an unexpected visit—I hope you aren't just going to stand there at the door and look at me. Sit down, won't you?"

He came forward, then, into the study. He went to the desk, opened a cigarette box of tooled leather and pushed it towards Ingram.

"Have a smoke?"

Ingram came slowly toward the desk. "No, thanks. I have my pipe. I came in to have a little talk with you, Luciano. I won't keep you up long, if you were thinking of turning in."

Luciano smiled, yawned a little behind the back of his hand and admitted: "I am a bit sleepy, professor. I've been running around a great deal lately."

Ingram nodded. "I've been looking for you since this morning and haven't been able to find you. You didn't attend your regular classes."

"No," Luciano said nonchalantly. "I had business that kept me away all day. You know how it is. A fellow's got to miss a few classes now and then."

Ingram began to fill his pipe. "That's not my concern," he said. "I'm not your dean. I'm not interested in what classes you may cut. I have something much more important to talk about."

"Have a seat," Luciano offered. Ingram went around the desk, drew out the swivel chair there and seated himself. Luciano pulled up another chair and sat down opposite. Still with his easy nonchalance he said: "What is it, professor? It must be terribly important if it brings you here at this hour."

Ingram assured him gravely: "It's probably the most important thing, Luciano, that you've ever discussed in your life."

For an instant, Luciano's face went sober, but then the smile reappeared.

"Just what is it?" he inquired.

Ingram lighted his pipe. "Luciano," he began, "I guess you know pretty well that I've been very deeply concerned in what's been going on these last two tragic days."

"Oh, we all have," Luciano stated, dropping his cigarette ash into a tray.

"Yes, I believe we have," Ingram agreed. "But some of us have been in it deeper than others, haven't we?"

A puzzled look came into Luciano's face. "Just what do you mean?" he asked quietly.

"Well, for my part," Ingram told him, "I discovered the body of Professor Yerkes. And then, on top of that, two very dear friends of mine became so involved that it's quite heart-sickening to me."

"I know," Luciano murmured sympathetically. "I'm so sorry."

"Their families, too," Ingram continued, "have become involved. Peace-loving people who have always shunned any kind of notoriety. It's a terrible thing, don't you think, Luciano?"

"It is, indeed."

"It was so terrible that I felt it was a matter not only for the police but for the good friends of those families to look into as well. And so, Luciano, I've done a little quiet investigating of my own during the past couple of days."

Luciano leaned forward. "Yes?"

"I'm hardly what you'd call a detective," Ingram went on. "My investigating has been simply a stumbling in the dark. But I did stumble toward something. You see, I started out with a theory. It was this: that Professor Yerkes had been murdered by someone whose past he was investigating. Professor Yerkes, you know, had done very well as an amateur detective. Now, from a little chat that I had with him some time ago, I became convinced that he was looking into the death of Professor Coombs. You know, Luciano, he wouldn't believe that Coombs committed suicide. He was convinced that it was murder. And he was looking for the murderer.

"And then—well, it is my opinion, Luciano, that he had discovered who the murderer was; that he confronted the murderer with the truth this past Wednesday and was then done to death to keep him silent on the subject of that murder."

"Yes?" Luciano murmured.

"Yes. Now, that theory made a certain course obvious. It meant that an investigation of the affairs of Professor Coombs would likely throw light on the identity of Yerkes's killer—as well as Coombs's."

"How ingenious!" Luciano exclaimed softly.

"Therefore," Ingram proceeded, "I looked into certain matters with which Professor Coombs had been concerned."

Luciano crushed out his cigarette, reached for another. He lighted up without removing his eyes from Ingram.

"I found," Ingram said, "some very vital tell-tale information in Coombs's effects."

"Is that so?"

"It is. Now, for a moment let me jump to another phase of the investigating that I did. At the beginning of this case there was a conflict, Luciano, between your word and Professor Bailey's. You stated that you placed your theme in the professor's box in Chatham House. Professor Bailey denied having been there, said that of course he had not taken out the theme. It was your word against his. But then circumstances took such a turn that Professor Bailey confessed a number of things. Besides confessing to the murder, he admitted opening his theme box and taking out your theme. I verified that statement, Luciano. He did have your theme. I found it, torn to pieces, in a wastebasket at Professor Bailey's home. I not only found it—I also put parts of it together."

"Proving that I had told the truth," Luciano put in.

"Yes. Now, on that theme paper, Luciano, there was written a telephone number in Professor Bailey's handwriting. It was written with an indelible lead pencil that was found on Professor Yerkes's desk, a pencil on which the fingerprints of Professor Bailey were found.

"Now, at first, Luciano, that telephone number didn't mean anything to me. I learned that it was the number of a certain woman named Maybelle Cunningham. That meant nothing to me. But then, to put what I told you at first in its proper chronological place, I examined Coombs's effects. There too, Luciano, I found that telephone number. The same number.

"I decided that here was a vital clue. I got the address of the Cunningham woman. I went there. I learned certain things. And I saw a certain person."

Ingram paused. Intent, no longer puffing his cigarette, Luciano sat stiff and erect in his chair.

"It was a certain person," Ingram went on, "that the newspapers like to describe as a very colorful character. It was one Joe Corvetti, overlord of all gangdom in the city. Corvetti, you might like to know, was a bootlegger when bootlegging was a big business. The outfit that he controls, a group of men with their headquarters in the city, runs dope, manipulates a large white slave traffic, handles crooked gambling enterprises, and is suspected of engineering some of the boldest kidnappings and murders in this part of the country."

"How terrible!" Luciano murmured.

Ingram knocked the coals out of his pipe into the tray on the desk.

"You're shocked?" he inquired. "Let me tell you something, Luciano, that shocked me even more than this seems to shock you. I had a brief but sufficient look at this Corvetti. In that single look I saw a resemblance to someone else, a very strong resemblance, a resemblance absolutely unmistakable. In the face of Joe Corvetti I saw the face of a person I knew. And I realized only too clearly then why, two days ago, District Attorney Bloomingdale wanted to know, Luciano, where he had seen you before. Luciano, it was your face I saw in Joe Corvetti's."

Luciano licked dry lips slowly. The expression in Ben Ingram's eyes was dark and menacing. He looked hardly at all like the genial, easy-going Ingram that students knew. He looked more like a killer himself. The look in his eyes was a sharp and dangerous look and his great hands that gripped the arms of the chair in which he sat were knotted and hard.

Luciano said in a dry, metallic voice: "Professor, I don't know what you're talking about."

"You wouldn't," Ingram said. "It would be your business not to know anything about all this except what you told so glibly to the police. Well, you aren't talking to the police now, Luciano. You aren't talking to the law at all. Or perhaps you are talking to the law—another kind of law—a law that will deal with you quite summarily if you can't find your tongue to speak the truth now.

"Luciano, Joe Corvetti is something to you. A brother, is my guess. Joe Corvetti is a murderer—and other things besides. Where Joe Corvetti's brother is, there we have a trail of blood and fear. The connection is quite apparent, Luciano—or Corvetti, or whatever your name really is. Somehow you and your precious brother are the perpetrators of all this tragedy that has come to us here. I don't pretend to know reasons. I don't need to know reasons. My mind is made up, Luciano, and unless you talk and talk fast, exercise some of the law that I carry in my own hands.

"Luciano, I want the truth out of you, or I'll strangle you with my bare hands and relish the job."

Ingram was almost out of the chair now. Luciano's look of nonchalance had become a dark, somber expression. He drew back slightly, his eyes fixed on Ingram.

"I'm waiting for you to talk," Ingram said grimly.

Luciano cleared his throat with a little nervous cough.

"Professor," he began, "I'm afraid you've gone quite insane. I'm beginning to think that you're the killer we've had here. Yes, it begins to look very much that way. Now, I warn you—"

"That'll be all of that cheap talk, Luciano!" Ingram was out of the chair. "Give me the truth, or you'll never talk again." He pushed back the chair and took a single step, coming around the corner of the desk.

Luciano cried sharply: "Professor, wait! You want the truth. All right—you'll get it. But don't whine afterwards that you didn't ask for it. Now, do as I say. Pick up that telephone and call the number I give you. You'll get the truth all right. Just sit down and call Glen Park 3287."

A new light came swiftly into Ingram's face. He stepped back, seated himself again and laid a hand upon the telephone.

"I've been waiting for exactly this," he said. And he picked up the receiver and dialed Glen Park 3287.

The humming dial tone ceased. There was a pause, then the buzzing sound of the ring at 3287. It sounded half a dozen times. Then a woman's voice answered.

"Hello. . . . Hello. . . ."

"Ask her to connect you with the penthouse," Luciano directed softly. "The penthouse."

"Connect me with the penthouse, please," Ingram said.

There was a soft click and another pause.

Then a man's voice said: "Hello! Hello! What is it? Who is it?"

Ingram looked at Luciano. Luciano stood up and reached for the telephone. Unhesitating, Ingram handed it to him.

"Hello," said Luciano. "Joe? Yes. . . . Yes, Joe. . . . I'm having trouble again, Joe. . . . What? . . . Yes, the same thing will work. The fellow's here. I'm going to give him the phone. You just tell him what'll happen to his girl if he doesn't keep his nose out of my business. I'm putting him on, Joe."

Luciano handed the telephone to Ingram. Eagerly Ingram took it out of his hands. Luciano's dark eyes were fixed upon him.

"Yes?" said Ingram into the instrument. "I'm listening."

"You're listening? All right—listen." The voice was hard, metallic, surprisingly like Luciano's. "I don't know who you are, Big Shot, and I don't care. But I guess you know who I am. I'm just telling you something, now, and I mean it. You play ball with the kid. You do as he says—see? You do just what he says. And if you don't, Big Shot, something's going to happen to that girl of yours—and it won't be anything very nice. It—won't—be—anything—very—nice. Get me? And if you don't think I'm talking turkey, just step out of line. Good-bye, rat!"

There was a click and the line was dead. Ingram was trembling as he set down the telephone.

"So that's the game," he said in a strained voice.

Luciano was looking at him with a faint, vicious smile.

"Believe me, professor," he said, and his voice was more than ever like the voice on the telephone, "believe me, it's no game. You'll mind your own business, professor, or something will happen to you and to Mary Bailey besides."

Ingram's hands were gripping the desk fiercely. "I get it, Luciano," he said. "I get every step of it now." He was on his feet, and started slowly around the desk toward Luciano. "But you've made one slip—one little slip." Luciano's brow clouded. "You've made one little omission, my friend. You didn't tell Corvetti who I was—and you didn't tell him who the girl was—and before you can tell him, Luciano, I'm going to kill you!"

Luciano's mouth fell open in horror. The sinister smile had vanished from his face, the sneer of mastery from his lips.

He laid his hands upon the arms of the chair as if to rise and protect himself, but Ingram's fingers were at his throat before he could get to his feet.

"Don't!" Luciano gasped. "In Heaven's name, don't!"

But Ingram was no longer a thinking, reasoning man. He was like an automaton with a single purpose, a purpose that he had no power to change. He was a killer now and before him was an evil life that must come to an end. The choking, gasping, half-paralyzed Luciano glared up at him.

"For God's sake!" he moaned. "Let me go!"

His words fell upon deaf ears. His voice died in a choked sob. He made a final effort to cry aloud.

Then the door to the room opened swiftly and quietly.

# 34
## FRIDAY 10 P.M.

The telephone rang in the round-table room of Joe Corvetti's penthouse. Corvetti, seated at the enormous table alone, answered it.

"The boys are here, Joe," a voice informed him. "Shall we come in?"

"Is that guy, the Professor, here?" Joe asked.

"No, he ain't here. Shall we come in anyhow?"

Joe Corvetti looked at his watch. It was several minutes before ten.

"Yeah, come in. I got a little preliminary business."

"Okay, Joe."

Joe hung up and resumed his perusal of several papers that lay before him; business reports. Business was good and Joe was pleased. There was only one thing wrong. They were short of machine guns, and you couldn't run business properly without machine guns. The shortage, however, was about to be taken care of.

Joe had been in touch with Coober. Coober, in the first instance, was a rat, but Coober was an ingenious mechanic. He could make guns, real guns, guns it was a pleasure to use, and now he was turning out something new, something light as a feather, and compact. Coober had once been a rival in business, but he was no man to run against Corvetti, and evidently Coober knew that, for he had retired from big business into the private and secret enterprise of gunmaking. He furnished guns to the underworld; guns made to order; guns made to any reasonable specification at all.

205

Coober was a good fellow, everything considered, and he carried no grudges. With Coober, business had been strictly business. If it had chanced that he had been crippled for life in one leg at Joe Corvetti's behest, Coober—as those who should know did know—had always accepted what had happened as part of the business he was in. And as the business had proved, in that incident, to be too strenuous for Coober, Coober had retired and left the field free and clear for Joe Corvetti. Corvetti appreciated this. He had told Coober so. He had told Coober that was why he was going to do right by him whenever he needed guns.

Coober was a man who said little. "I make good guns," he said, and shrugged.

Joe Corvetti perused his papers.

Corvetti was a man who had made a great deal of money and who liked good things in lavish measure. His magnificent penthouse headquarters—one of several establishments—were atop a fifty-story building. The height made Joe feel like a god over the rest of mankind. In his own estimation he was more or less like a deity. He had the power of life and death in his hands and even in the nod of his head. He had only to gesture in the direction of someone who should live no longer and that person was swiftly and mysteriously done to death.

Joe's angels of death and cooperation were fourteen. Joe believed in a comparatively small, compact outfit controlled completely by himself, yet composed of men who had a share and a say in the many complicated businesses that the outfit ran. Joe was a business man to the finger tips. No loose organization would suit him. Their group was a kind of corporation. The members bought in—provided they were the right kind to have as members—and they shared in the profits according to the size of their respective interests, and voted in the questions that came up for consideration.

Any matter that had anything to do with the business, any matter that required the possession of information incriminating to the outfit, was handled by one of the fifteen—by no one else. In the handling of a certain item of business, an incidental killing might be necessary. There was no man among these fifteen who had any scruples about doing a good practical killing with his own hands, if it were necessary. But it was permissible, under the rules of the organization, for a member to delegate such routine and bloody work to a hireling. That hireling, however, would never know any more than the fact that he was being paid to take a designated person for a ride. Oftenest he did not know even who hired him to do it. All he knew was that he got his money in advance—good pay, too—and that he had better do the job if he knew what was good for him.

Corvetti pushed aside his batch of papers as the door to the round-table room opened. The men straggled in, one at a time. Some of them looked like the type of ordinary business man who goes downtown every morning to work in an office; some of them looked tough as rawhide; some of them were sleek and smooth dandies; two of them were indisputably handsome. Fourteen of them. "Hello, Joe." "Evening, Joe." "How's your health, Joe?" "Well, Joe, how's tricks?" Joe nodded and lifted a hand in greeting. The men stood around, chatting softly. One, standing across the large table from Corvetti, asked: "Where's the new typewriters, Joe? Here yet?"

"The guy ought to be here in a minute," Joe said. "I told 'em ten o'clock. Coober's sending a mug he calls the Professor. He's gonna do the demonstrating. Coober's got something new in Tommy guns— something you can put in your vest pocket, I guess."

"Good. We can use 'em all right. How many are you taking?"

"All we can get, if they're the goods."

"Hm! Sounds like business is going to expand."

"It is."

"Going to try it out on the range?"

"Sure. That's what the range is for, ain't it?"

"Sure."

Joe raised his voice. "All right. Fill the seats. We've got a little preliminary business before the big show."

The men strolled up to their seats, sat down leisurely, smoking, talking. The table was so large that their fifteen chairs, placed not more than a foot apart, went scarcely a third of the way around, forming an arc of the best material that organized crime had to offer in that part of the country. Joe was at the head of the table. On each side of him sat seven.

The meeting came to order. Thereupon, Joe Corvetti sat back in his seat and told his organization what was wrong with it. He told his white-slave gentlemen where they were wrong, his dope manipulators what was the matter with them. He was just about to inform his robbery experts of their chief faults and to tell them that the new Tommy gun was for their especial benefit, when the telephone rang again.

Joe Corvetti answered. "Hello."

"This is the Professor," said a voice.

"Yeah? Well, come right up." He put up the receiver, glanced at his watch.

"Ten minutes late," he complained. "Well, we'll listen to his spiel here. Then we'll go over to the range."

The range was at the far end of the roof. It was a sound-proofed structure in which Corvetti and his gangsters tried out guns and practiced to keep eye and finger in condition.

A buzzer over the door sounded. Joe pressed a button under the table. The door clicked, then opened. All the men at the table turned their eyes to that door.

"Hello," said Corvetti. "Come in."

The man who came in was tall and thin. His face was pale, gray; his eyes blue, cold, hard.

"So you're the Professor?" Corvetti asked.

The man cleared his throat. "That's right. Coober sent me."

He wore a gray topcoat and a gray hat and carried a black valise. He came forward across the room and stood before the table, directly opposite Joe Corvetti. His eyes went slowly about the arc of men.

"You want this gun demonstrated," he said. "That's what Coober said."

"That's the story." Corvetti nodded. "And we want to know how many we can have, if it's satisfactory."

"You can have all you want. That's what Coober said."

"Okay. If the price is right."

"The price will be right. Coober said so."

"All right. Let's see it."

The Professor laid the valise on the table, opened two straps, lifted the cover. He took out a small, compact sub-machine gun.

"Coober says to tell you that this is—that it's his masterpiece. He says there's nothing better anywhere. Sure action. Can't jam. Light as a feather. Coober calls it the Featherbaby."

Corvetti grinned. "Not a bad name."

"No," said the Professor, "not a bad name."

"Okay. Now let's have a look at it."

The Professor nodded. He took the gun in one hand. It was neat, easy to carry. The Professor stepped back.

"Let's have a look at it," Corvetti repeated.

Then the telephone rang. Corvetti reached for it.

## 35
### FRIDAY 10:20 P.M.

"Hello," said Corvetti. "Hello! What is it? Who is it?"

There was a pause. A frown came over Corvetti's features.

"Who's that? You, kid? I'm in conference, kid. Make it snappy. What's that? You're having trouble? The same business? Will the same thing work? If it will, you know you can count on me. Where's the guy? Got him there? Put him on. What do I tell this one?"

There was another pause. Then Corvetti said: "You're listening? All right—listen. I don't know who you are, Big Shot, and I don't care. But I guess you know who I am. I'm just telling you something, now, and I mean it. You play ball with the kid. You do as he says—see? You do just what he says. And if you don't, Big Shot, something's going to happen to that girl of yours— and it won't be anything very nice. It—won't—he—anything— very—nice. Get me? And if you don't think I'm talking turkey, just step out of line. Good-bye, rat!"

Corvetti hung up. For a few moments he sat with his hand on the telephone. Then he looked up at the Professor again.

"Now, Professor," he began.

The Professor had backed away from the round table. He had turned a very ghastly white and his eyes were fixed on Joe Corvetti. He held the gun firmly in both hands now, almost as if he intended to use it.

"What's the matter, Professor?" Corvetti asked. "You look sick. Something you ate? Have a little drink. It'll settle you."

The Professor's lips moved nervously. Then he said:

"Corvetti, who was that you were threatening?"

Corvetti scowled. Every face at the table was turned in surprise toward the Professor.

"Who was I threatening?" Corvetti echoed. "I wasn't threatening anybody, Professor. And unless you're a little goofy, you ought to know that you aren't here to ask questions but to answer them. What's it to you, anyhow? Say," and Corvetti pushed his chair back a little from the table, "who are you anyhow? Are you here to sell me guns or ain't you?"

The Professor backed away another step. He held the gun waist high now, and his finger was on the trigger. The fourteen and their leader sat frozen in astonishment, staring at this crazy-looking old man who dared to point a gun at them.

One of the fourteen said: "Hey, what is this? This guy's goofy. What's up, chief?"

And Corvetti said: "Listen, Professor. Put that gun down before it goes off. If you're nervous for a little shot of powder, I'll see you get it. Come on, now, Professor, bring the gun up and let me see it."

The Professor said in a thin, hard voice: "I can handle the gun very well from here, thank you. And it's from here that I intend to use it. I—"

"What the hell!" one of the men cried. "This is a stickup! I'll—"

"The only thing you'll do, young man," the Professor said, his eyes fixed not on the one who had spoken, but still on Corvetti, "is put your hands up over your head. And that's good advice for all of you. Yes, all of you had better put your hands up over your heads. If any of you reach for a weapon, I'll demonstrate the Featherbaby and leave no doubt as to its efficiency. Up with them, gentlemen! Put your hands up and put them up high."

An oath exploded from Corvetti's lips.

"Coober!" he cried. "That rat framed this. This is no—"

"Over your head," said the Professor. "I'm especially interested in you, Corvetti. Put them up high, please. Now, stand up. Every one of you, stand up!"

Almost with one accord the fifteen men rose slowly from their chairs.

"What do you want?" Corvetti demanded. "What are you up to? What the hell is this?"

The Professor ignored the questions. "You will all back away from the table," he ordered, "and form a line at that end of the room, facing me. You will start moving now—and keep your hands high."

"This is the spot!" one of the men cried. "We're on the spot, I tell you!"

"You ain't on any spot," Corvetti growled. "Nobody puts us on the spot. This is a stickup—ain't it, Professor? Ain't it a stickup?"

"It's a stickup all right," the Professor assured him. "Keep backing away, please—clear of the table. . . . There! . . . There! That'll do. Now, stand still."

The fifteen men stood in line. Some were calm, others were pale and shaking. One of them gasped: "Who is this guy? What's he want? What's he—"

In a strangely clear voice, the Professor said:

"You want to know what I want? I'll tell you. I'll tell you what I want. I want peace and safety for mankind. I want unendangered homes, unendangered wives and children. I want peace of mind for them and safety for their persons. I want no more murder and fear, slaughter and horror, rule by intimidation and terror. I want no more blocking of justice, no more ruling of our lives by a stinking underworld. I want freedom and light, joy and happiness, right-living and right-thinking—peace—peace—peace—you rats! I know a step towards all this. It is to eliminate the enemies of it. You are the enemies. Say your prayers—for I shall eliminate you!"

"For God's sake!" one of the men cried. "This guy's cracked as a—"

"Shut up!" Corvetti snapped. "Look here, Professor—"

But the Professor had time for no more words. He took a single step forward now and the little Featherbaby began to chatter. A swift, choking chatter.

The men in the line cried out. Some dropped their hands in desperation, seeking weapons. The Featherbaby fanned back and forth. Its awful, scorching breath withered the line of fifteen men. They crumpled and fell, choking, gasping, swearing. Corvetti went down on his knees as the bullets ripped into him.

"Get that guy!" he choked. "Somebody get him!" And fell forward on his face.

The fifteen were down, but still the gun blazed and sprayed back and forth upon them.

In a last desperate effort a head raised itself from the tangled limbs and a hand came slowly up, lifting an automatic gun. The hand wavered, steadied, and the gun spoke—once, twice.

Both shots struck the Professor in the chest. He staggered back. The Featherbaby fell out of his hands with a clatter. A little moan on his lips, the Professor collapsed, fell toward the Featherbaby and lay quite still, one outstretched hand grasping the warm barrel.

# 36
## SATURDAY 9:30 A.M.

Captain Packer, who had spent one of the busiest nights of his whole official career, sat in Johnny Mortimer's office in the court house. Mortimer had been out of town on a case and had just got in on the early morning train. Together, Mortimer and Packer scanned the headlines of the morning papers.

"My God!" Mortimer said. "I never saw anything like it! Those headlines are like a blast of dynamite!"

"The whole thing is a blast of dynamite," the captain said soberly.

The headlines blared:

CORVETTI GANG WIPED OUT!
ST. VALENTINE'S DAY MURDERS
PUT IN SHADE
STUDENT LUCIANO CONFESSES
UNIVERSITY KILLINGS
University Professor Annihilates Corvetti Group—
Professor Davis Dying from Bullet Wounds—
Luciano Linked With Corvetti Mob—
Brother of Gangster-Chief Dilettante
University Student—
Professor Ingram's
Amazing Detective Work

## CORVETTI ORGANIZATION SLAUGHTERED!
### UNIVERSITY STUDENT CONFESSES KILLINGS
University Mystery Smashed Wide Open—
Amazing Gangster Tie-Up
Avenging Professor Slaughters
Gangsters with Machine Gun
Professor Dying from Gangster's Bullets
Only Two Shots Fired by Gangsters
Tricked by Professor Davis

Mortimer pushed away the papers.

"To hell with those!" he said. "Give me the first-hand dope. Here all this goes on and I have to be out of town! Come on, captain; you saw it all."

"Sure," said the captain. "And I was up all night, too, doing it. All right. Sit down. I'll tell you and then I'll go home and sleep it off."

Mortimer thrust a panatela at the captain and gave him a light. "I'm listening," he said. "How did it all break?"

Packer puffed slowly on the cigar. "Well," he began, "before I tell you how it all broke, let me tell you—just between you and me—what I think of the whole bunch of us: you and Bloomingdale and myself and everybody else that worked officially on the case. We're a bunch of boobs. We turned down every straight, plain lead and fell for everything we shouldn't have. And gummed everything up aplenty. And it took a nice, easy-going college professor, who doesn't know the first thing about police work, to do what real detective work was done. I mean Ingram."

"And you had a suspicion or two about Ingram, didn't you?" Mortimer asked.

The captain held up a hand. "Don't let it get any further," he said.

"Go on," Mortimer urged.

The captain grinned sheepishly. "It seems to come right back to the same thing—that we were beginning to think Ingram was in on it somewhere. Bloomingdale and I went over to his place yesterday. We thought maybe Davis was hiding out there. Well,

Ingram got up on his dignity for the first time. We didn't go through the house, but we put a man on his tail. Harlan.

"Well, he didn't do much that was important until ten o'clock last night. He went then to Luciano's place. Harlan followed and listened outside the door. Well, you never heard anything like what happened inside there. The professor accused Luciano of being the killer and being tied up with Joe Corvetti, and when Luciano wouldn't talk, Ingram decided to take the law into his own hands. He was just about strangling Luciano when Harlan stepped in and put a stop to it.

"Well, we brought Luciano down here and gave him the works. And just then the story broke about what went on in Corvetti's place. Mortimer, you could have knocked me over with a feather. And when Luciano heard about it, it finished him. He went to pieces and told the whole story.

"Now, the uncanny part of the whole thing is that Ingram had it all figured out cold before Luciano broke down. He told us just what he thought even before Luciano confessed. Here's the way he had worked on it. Get this if you want a little lesson in investigating.

"It seems Ingram never believed, from the very first, that either Bailey or Davis had anything to do with killing Yerkes. Knowledge of character—that kind of stuff. Said he had known them since he was a kid. Knew they weren't capable of anything like that. Worked on that basis. Not such a bad basis, it seems; at any rate, not so bad in this case.

"Well, Ingram started out with a theory. And if you want to know, we had the same material right in our own hands at the start of the case and even talked it over. It had to do with Yerkes's investigation, his puttering around in what they called the university mysteries.

"You remember this Professor Coombs that committed suicide here about a year ago? Shot himself through the head. Remember the case? Well, Ingram was of the opinion that Yerkes was looking into that case. He'd had a talk with Yerkes some time before his death, and Yerkes evidently told Ingram he didn't believe Coombs killed himself. Well, that was all Ingram had to indicate that Yerkes was working on the Coombs case, but he thought it was enough to start a theory on. He figured that, on the afternoon Yerkes was killed, when he left that note under the door, he wanted to tell Ingram what he had learned. It seems he had done that very thing before when he finished a case and wanted to talk it over with some one.

"But, Ingram figured, the killer got to Yerkes before Ingram did. So, you see, Ingram argued that the one who killed Coombs was the one who killed Yerkes too. And as the leads in the Yerkes killing were none too good, and the police were hogging everything and keeping everybody else off—which they were—he decided to see if there wasn't anything to learn, in the first instance, about who killed Coombs. He told himself that if Yerkes had found clues leading to the Coombs killer, maybe he could stumble over the same clues. Modest feller. He didn't do any stumbling, the way I see it.

"Well, Ingram set out to find out something about what had gone on in Coombs's home life. It seems Coombs had lived with his daughter, a girl named Jacqueline—a fine girl, she was; a sort of semi-invalid—and they had a housekeeper by the name of Mrs. Garrett. Well, a little over a year ago, the daughter died. For a little while Coombs lived on in the house with only the housekeeper. And then one day they found him dead and pronounced him suicide. Shot through the right side of the head.

"Well, Ingram went over to have a talk with this Mrs. Garrett. She lives in a little place of her own just outside the university area. Ingram put the thing straight to her and asked her if she could help in any way. She denied knowing a thing that would point toward murder instead of suicide and she got all upset about it and asked Ingram to get out. Which he did.

"Then he came over here and got Bloomingdale's permission to talk with Bailey in his cell. Bailey told his story to Ingram just as he told it to us, and Ingram, clever feller, told Bailey he didn't believe he'd have stopped to open his theme box if he came over expressly to kill—as he said he did. And right there Ingram put his finger on the chief defect in Bailey's confession, which none of us had brains enough to see.

"Well, the next thing Ingram does is to go over to the Bailey house and see if he can locate Luciano's theme paper among Bailey's things. And find it they did—he and Mary Bailey—in a wastebasket, torn up. They put it together and on it what do you think they found? A telephone number written with indelible lead pencil—in Professor Bailey's handwriting.

"Now, Ingram knew Yerkes kept indelible pencils on his desk. So he began putting two's together and figured out what looked like a pretty good four. He learned from Bloomingdale that we'd found an indelible pencil on Yerkes's desk with Bailey's fingerprints on it. That told him that Bailey had been in Yerkes's office, and tallied with the confession about getting the theme out of the box and then going upstairs to Yerkes's place; but still Ingram wasn't satisfied. He admits he was stumped on the confession angle by this time and he gave that a rest.

"Then the next intelligent thing he did was to get the listing on the phone number—Glen Park 3287. And though he didn't know it right off, that's where he stepped on the biggest lead of all.

"Then he had an appointment to see Coombs's executor. That was another smart move. He wanted to know if he could find anything in Coombs's effects that would give him a clue. He learned from the executor, a man named Blanding, that Yerkes had been there on the same mission a while before. And what do you think Ingram stumbled on to on one of the papers? Well, it was a paper with a lot of figures on it and down at the bottom of the page he found the same phone number, Glen Park 3287.

"First thing in the morning, then,—yesterday morning—he went down to the address where the phone was listed, and he inquired. He found out that the party—a woman—was the girlfriend of Corvetti the gangster, and while he was still there Corvetti came out and Ingram got a look at him. And right away spotted the resemblance to Luciano.

"You know, by golly, Mortimer, it's a wonder one of us smart guys never thought of that resemblance. Now, you went down to interview Corvetti—"

"Yes," Mortimer put in, "but you forget I never saw Luciano. I didn't come on this job until after he'd been questioned at the beginning, and I wasn't around at any other time when he showed up."

The captain nodded. "Anyway," he went on, "Bloomingdale almost got it—but almost isn't enough. Bloomingdale thought he looked like somebody, but he couldn't think who. Well, there's Ingram, hot on Luciano's trail. He had begun to figure that Luciano's story was trumped up in some way; that what he told about just stepping into Chatham House, dropping in the theme and leaving almost at once was just a cover-up. So he looked for Luciano, found him last night, called his bluff and got introduced to the phone number for the third time. Luciano told him to call up and ask to be put through to Corvetti. When Corvetti came on, he told Ingram to keep his hands off the kid or something would happen to Ingram's girl. Right then, Ingram decided to do a little murdering himself. And Harlan stopped him just in time."

"Whew!" Mortimer exclaimed. "Then what?"

"Well, we got Luciano here and gave him the works. Then the news broke about the Corvetti massacre and he went up in the air, opened up and spilled everything. Listen to this for sweet and gentle extortion.

"He came to college here to make a gentleman out of himself. Joe Corvetti's been sending him to good schools ever since he was a kid, but every now and then he'd cut loose and get himself mixed up in some kind of bad business or other. Just a bad egg, that's all. And every time he got in dutch, Corvetti straightened him out.

"Well, it seems about a year ago he was in need of a little extra cash, and instead of going to Corvetti for it, he decided to run a little business of his own. He began to put the bee on old Professor Coombs. I guess he had the old guy scared stiff. He told him if he didn't come across, something would happen to his daughter, Jacqueline. And he said if Coombs went to the police that would finish things for the daughter. He let Coombs know he was tied up with Corvetti, and Corvetti must have told him to play ball with Luciano or else. So Luciano had the old boy doing just what he wanted. He milked him for plenty. The list of figures Ingram found in Blanding's office was an account of the money that had been paid to Luciano from time to time, in cash.

"Then the daughter died and Coombs wasn't afraid anymore. The next time Luciano asked for cash, Coombs told him the game was up and that he was going to turn him over to the police; that he didn't give a hoot what happened to himself now that the girl, Jacqueline, was gone. So Luciano let him have it—with Coombs's own gun—and fixed it up to look like suicide. And here's where the housekeeper comes in.

"It seems she heard what went on in Coombs's study just before the old feller got his. And it also seems that she knew something about the extortion that was going on and the tie-up with Corvetti's mob; but she was afraid to open her mouth lest they get her for it.

"Well, after the death was pronounced suicide, Yerkes, working on the case over several months, figured out the truth of it. Exactly how he did it we'll never know; but he did it. Then, the afternoon of his death, he went to his office in Chatham House, after leaving the note for Ingram to come upstairs. He called up Luciano and asked him to come over. Luciano came over. He brought the theme with him, dropped it in the box and went upstairs to see Yerkes.

"Yerkes laid out the facts, accused Luciano of killing Coombs and was going to call the police. Luciano tried to pull the Glen Park number on him, but Yerkes wouldn't bite. So Luciano, who was carrying a gun, let him have it right across the desk.

"Now—there were other people in the building. Usually the place is deserted on Wednesday—no conferences and such. But it happened that there were three people there right at that time. Upstairs, on the same floor with Yerkes, Bailey and Davis were each in their separate offices. Downstairs, in one of the study rooms, was the student Crane. All three heard the shot.

"Now, Davis had been there for some time. Bailey had come in shortly after Luciano deposited his theme—two-thirty or thereabouts. Bailey had taken out the theme and gone upstairs to his office. When he heard the shot, he came out, and met Davis in the corridor. They went down to Yerkes's office together and walked in. Luciano greeted them with his gun.

"Well, it was a pretty desperate moment for everybody. Why Luciano didn't let them have it too, I don't know. Anyhow, what he did was this. He told Bailey to call up that number. Scared, confused, Bailey pulled a paper out of his pocket—Luciano's theme—and wrote down the number with a pencil from Yerkes's desk. Then he made the call and got put through to Corvetti, and Corvetti told him to do as Luciano said or what would happen not only to himself and Davis but also to Mary Bailey and Mrs. Davis wouldn't be very pretty. The scare they threw into Bailey and Davis was aplenty, I tell you. The two of them swore they'd never tell a word.

"Then Luciano went downstairs and out; and that's when Ingram met him. Bailey and Davis beat it by way of the back door, afraid they'd meet someone coming in the front way and have to do a little explaining. They got away unseen except for the janitor, and went back to their homes.

"Just at what instant Crane got out of there, I'm not sure. It must have been while Ingram was on the upper corridor, just before he broke into Yerkes's office.

"Well, Luciano thought he was safe. But then, later in the day, he had a talk with Crane. Crane, it seems, knew what it was all about. He'd heard enough. He was badly frightened. Luciano was worried that we might get Crane on the carpet and force the story out of him. So what did he do? He got Corvetti to put the finger on him. Corvetti sent out Tark to do the job—and he did it.

"Now we come to the reaction of Bailey and Davis. Their first decision to say nothing was, of course, based on the hope that no one would know they had been there. When we found out they had been there, what do we get? Bailey confesses, accepts the entire guilt himself; would even, I believe, have gone to the chair rather than jeopardize his daughter's safety by telling the truth and involving Luciano.

"Davis, in the meantime, made himself scarce. He talked at the hospital last night and told just what his reaction was. He decided that he was not going to let the blame for this fall upon Bailey. And he says he came to the realization that the only way to get Bailey to tell the truth was to annihilate the menace to Mary Bailey, to Mrs. Davis and to every one else concerned. He knew from what had happened to Crane that Luciano and Corvetti meant business. So Davis set out to meet and beat Corvetti at his own game.

"He got himself a machine gun somewhere. He was meeting someone and making arrangements to get the gun at the time Maguire lost him in that vacant house, the time he was with Jerry the Pole. Well, he got the gun—we still don't know where he got it—and he had some arrangement made, heaven knows how, to get into Corvetti's place when they were having a full meeting of the outfit. Well, he got in, lined them up and drilled every one of them. That, Mortimer, just between you and me, was a masterpiece. It was probably just the thing that many a self-respecting citizen has wished he had nerve enough and cleverness enough, and probably cooperation enough, to do. Mortimer, every last one of Corvetti's outfit is gone, dead as a doornail.

"Davis himself probably won't pull through. When I left the hospital just a little while ago, his wife was sitting there by his side, holding his hand. They'd told her the whole story and the poor old soul just sat there with a smile on her face—a smile, mind you—and told them how proud she was of her man. She's a nice person, Mortimer. I feel damned sorry for her."

The captain paused, took out his handkerchief and patted his moist brow.

Mortimer asked: "Did Bailey say what it was that came through the window just before he confessed?"

"Yes. Luciano wrote a warning, tied it around a stone and chucked it in from down below. It touched Bailey's panic off. He was in bad shape as it was. He went into that terrible screaming hysteria and came through with his confession. And, mind you, Luciano chucked it in while he was on his way from his room to Chatham House to report that he'd been shot at."

"Oh, yes. Who'd shot at him? Davis?"

"No. He fired that shot himself. He'd begun to realize that probably some smart cop might figure he wasn't as innocent as he pretended to be. So he decided to make it look as if someone was after his hide too. He smudged the window in his room, fired the shot at the wall and then put up his bluff about being scared. Clever, while it lasted."

Mortimer scratched his head thoughtfully.

"What gets me more than anybody's cleverness in this thing," he said, "is what those two old profs did when they saw they were up against it. One goes to take the murder rap to protect his daughter. The other walks into the lion's den and lets him have it— to protect his wife and incidentally to nullify his friend's confession. Say, captain, you and I will have to remember this case every time we have a confession or a fugitive. Maybe it'll teach us everything isn't what it seems, and that we aren't so darned smart after all."

"You're telling me?" said the captain. "The trouble is, next time we'll be just as smart and we'll be hollering spades are spades even before we turn the cards over to see what they are."

# 37
## SATURDAY—NOON

Mary Bailey answered the bell at Ingram's ring. She opened it and he stepped in. She threw her arms about his neck and kissed him, and the joy of the moment seemed to sweep away the tragedy of these days.

"Oh, Ben!" she cried. "They've told me all about it. They've told me that you were the only real detective in this case. They've told me how cleverly—"

"Nonsense!" said Ingram. "If there's anybody to thank or praise, it is—it was, Mary—Tad Davis. He died just now."

"Oh, no, Ben!"

"Yes. And she sits there beside him and says over and over that she's so proud of him. It's heart breaking. We'll have to do a great deal for her, Mary. We'll have to take care of her—just as long as she lives. I think she'll bear up. I thought she'd go to pieces—collapse—but she didn't. She sits there, holding his hand and saying that she's going to be strong for his sake. He asked her to do that, Mary, with his very last breath."

Mary wept softly on Ingram's shoulder. He led her gently into the living room and they sat side by side in silence for a long time.

"Your father," he asked at length, "how is he?"

"He's all right," she replied. "Dr. Royal made him get into bed, gave him something to make him sleep. When he has some rest and gets his strength back, he'll be all right. He was terribly upset about Uncle Tad."

"I know. I think, Mary, that as soon as he's able, he ought to get away from here for a while. It'll help him to get all this out of his mind."

"Yes. And I think," she added, "it would do all of us a great deal of good to get away. You and I ought to—don't you think?"

"You mean—?"

"Yes," she said. "But I'm not going to let you ask me to marry you for the tenth time. I'm asking you, and I want it soon; right away, Ben; as soon as everything is straightened out. I don't want to be without you any more. I never knew till now how terribly I need you. Please say yes, Ben."

He smiled, took her in his arms again, kissed her.

"It is a great honor to accept your proposal," he told her.

He grinned happily now, brushed away fresh tears that started down her cheeks and met her lips again as she raised them to his.

**COACHWHIP PUBLICATIONS**
COACHWHIPBOOKS.COM

A JUDGE MASSIE MYSTERY

# THE CORPSE IS INDIGNANT

DOUGLAS STAPLETON
and HELEN A. CAREY

COACHWHIP PUBLICATIONS
COACHWHIPBOOKS.COM

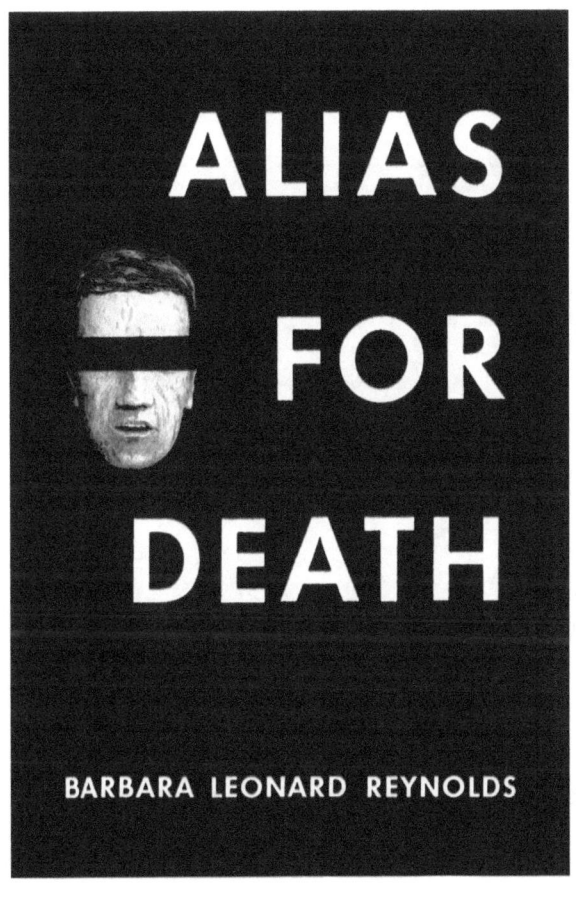

MURDER TAKES
THE VEIL

MURDER AT
ST. DENNIS

SISTER SIMON'S
MURDER CASE

THE MARGARET ANN HUBBARD
MYSTERY OMNIBUS

**COACHWHIP PUBLICATIONS**
CoachwhipBooks.com

THE
SARA ELIZABETH
MASON
MYSTERIES

*MURDER RENTS A ROOM*

*THE CRIMSON FEATHER*

# COACHWHIP PUBLICATIONS
## CoachwhipBooks.com

THE
SARA ELIZABETH
MASON
MYSTERIES

THE HOUSE THAT HATE BUILT

⫸ ⫷

THE WHIP

COACHWHIP PUBLICATIONS
COACHWHIPBOOKS.COM

# THE GOLDFISH MURDERS

WILL MITCHELL

COACHWHIP PUBLICATIONS

CoachwhipBooks.com

NARROW
GAUGE TO
MURDER

Carolyn Thomas

www.ingramcontent.com/pod-product-compliance
Lightning Source LLC
Chambersburg PA
CBHW020640260626
47157CB00008B/2842